A SUDDEN PASSING

BLYTHE BAKER

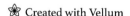 Created with Vellum

A sinister plot unveiled...

Rose Beckingham's pursuit of an international assassin leads her to New York City, where she reunites with her cousins from London. But danger follows Rose across the Atlantic and it's not long before she must confront shadows from her past.

As she races against time to save a life, will the arrival of a familiar face hinder her investigation or offer a vital clue?

1

When Catherine's letter arrived from New York, I expected it to be in response to my letter. The one I had sent only weeks before, detailing that her aunt and uncle had been killed in a bombing that, far from being an accident, had actually been a planned assassination on Mr. Beckingham with no mercy shown to his family or servants. It had been difficult news to deliver—and news that had been difficultly fought for—but she and the rest of her family deserved to know the true fate of their loved ones.

"A letter for you, Miss Rose," Jalini said, her dark skin glowing from time spent outdoors in the summer heat. She handed me the envelope and studied my face as I read it. "Is it the letter you've been expecting?"

"Is it obvious I've been expecting something?" I asked.

"You have met me in the entrance hall each of the last three afternoons, so I only assumed you were waiting for something," she said. "Is it in regards to Mr. Barlow?"

"Do not call him that," I snapped, somewhat unfairly,

before taking a breath and continuing in a calmer manner. "I do not know his true identity, but that name did not belong to him."

I'd done my best not to dwell on Mr. Barlow in the weeks since our encounter. He was responsible for so much of the chaos of my previous year, and I did not want to allow him another second of my time. Especially when my time could be much better spent trying to uncover the identity of Mr. Barlow's boss, The American. The mysterious man who had named Mr. Beckingham as a target to begin with. I had managed to dispose of Mr. Barlow, so in addition to being an unsavory thought, he was also a wasted one.

Jalini bowed her head in apology. "Forgive me."

"No, forgive me," I sighed, tucking the letter from my cousin against my chest. "You were instrumental in leading me to Mr. Barlow as the killer, so you should feel free to refer to him as you'd like. I suppose I am still sensitive to mention of him."

"And you, Miss Rose, were instrumental in ensuring Mr. Barlow caused no one in this home any harm, so I will not say anything about him that would upset you," she said, backing away towards the servant's hallway.

I smiled in thanks as she left, and then raced up the stairs before I could be stopped again.

Mr. and Mrs. Hutchins had rebounded remarkably well after the discovery that Mr. Hutchins' personal assistant was an international assassin sent to murder him. I'd expected the discovery to have some kind of marked change on their behavior. Perhaps, Mrs. Hutchins would discover a new zest for life and leave the library more than for meal times. Maybe Mr. Hutchins would speak with his peers in the government and forge connections that would see him spending less time with his mother. But neither happened. Mrs. Hutchins spent more time than ever in the library, aggressively waving a folded fan in front of her to combat the "oppressive" heat, and Mr. Hutchins distracted himself by interviewing a long string of personal secretaries who all marched through the house at all hours of the day and night.

Mrs. Hutchins found the parade of potential employees to be inconvenient, and Mr. Hutchins found his mother's nagging to be excessive. And both of them believed me to be the greatest listener they knew. Mrs. Hutchins cornered me whenever possible to rage against her son's disrespectful behavior, and even Mr. Hutchins, who had never much cared for me, took to complaining about his mother whenever we found ourselves alone. I suspected Mr. Barlow had been his listening ear prior to his death and the reveal that he had been betraying the Hutchinses for the entire duration of his employment.

As I walked down the hallway to my room, I could hear Mrs. Hutchins instructing a servant to open the library window, and I darted past the open door before she could see me. As soon as I made it to my room, I closed the door quietly, walked to my desk, and slid Catherine's note out of the envelope. It was neatly written in a tight, curling script.

DEAREST ROSE,
    Alice and I swore we would never forgive you after you

promised to accompany us to New York, but instead travelled to India with a man, but you'll be happy to know we have both forgiven you. I admit, my anger lasted longer than Alice's. She heard a detailed description of the man you left with, and she understood your motivations at once. It seems you have confided in her more than in me. She asks that I send her regards to this Monsieur Prideaux, so do see that he receives those. My forgiveness came more slowly. It will shock you to hear me say so, but I have not always been a compassionate woman, nor one of understanding. Because I wanted to go to New York, I could not understand why the same would not be true of you. However, I have met someone since coming to the city who has helped me to see otherwise. While listening to my frustrations towards my cousin, he placed himself in your shoes and wondered whether the trauma of your past required a grand adventure to move on. He suspected settling down amongst family would allow too much time for contemplation, and I forgave you at once. For being in New York has given me far too much time to think. About you and your parents, about my previous relationships, and of Edward. I have spent hours looking over my sins and mistakes, wondering where I could have done something differently to change the outcomes. I can now see why you might not have wanted to devote the same amount of time to your thoughts. The man you can send your thanks to for my improvement is Charles Cresswell.

I would ask if you know of him, but he assures me you two have never met. He is a British diplomat working at the embassy in New York, and our meeting was both chance and fate—Alice is insisting I cut the story of our meeting short because she has heard it too many times and wants to know the ending of this letter before she must leave for a meeting of her friends. As you can see, she is just as incorrigible and silly as ever. To keep it brief, Charles Cresswell and I are engaged. He has always been a good man, and I wish for you to come meet him at once in order to make your own determination on the matter.

There are many reasons you could give to not make the trip. It is costly and time-consuming, quite uncomfortable no matter how nice the ship, and you have done a great deal of travelling in the last year. However, your presence here is vital to my happiness. It is the only reason I have for begging you to come, and I pray it will be enough to convince you.

I await your response and arrival eagerly.

Love,

Catherine

NO MENTION OF MR. BARLOW. No mention of my near-death experience. Of the deaths of the Beckinghams at the hands of a madman. Clearly, Catherine was distracted by other matters.

Going back to New York City was something I had come to dread for many reasons, most of them revolving around my disguise as Rose Beckingham. New York City had been the home of Nellie Dennet, a woman who was now gone, assumed dead in the Simla bombing, but who shared my face nonetheless. Going back to New York risked my cover. If I ran into someone I knew from my old life, it could unravel the tapestry of lies I'd so carefully woven. Not to mention, New York City was where I had lost my real family. It was where my real parents were murdered, where my brother was suspected of the crime and had abandoned me to run. It was where what little innocence that remained of my childhood was stripped away, leaving me destitute on the streets. New York City was where the events that would lead me to the Beckinghams, to the bombing, and to a life of impersonating my dead friend would begin. Was I truly ready to go back there?

All of that aside, another question plagued me. Why did my cousin wish for my company? Catherine and I had never been particularly close, and now that she was set to be married, she would have little need for my company. I would have imagined her too infatuated with her soon-to-be husband to care about her missing cousin. And yet, she wrote to ask me, nay, *beg me* to come to New York. Why?

Your presence here is vital to my happiness.

I read the letter again and could not decide whether my own proclivity for mysteries made the words seem more ominous than they were intended or whether the words were pointing towards trouble in the union.

He has always been a good man, and I wish for you to come meet him at once in order to make your own determination on the matter.

If my cousin did need my help, could I refuse? Or what if I crossed an ocean only to discover I had read trouble into what was nothing more than a wedding announcement? There was always the option to write back and ask outright, but if Catherine had chosen discretion in this letter, I had no reason to believe she would wish to be more forthcoming in another. Besides, what was in Simla for me now?

Mrs. Hutchins and her son had accepted me into their home and lives, but I could not live on their kindness forever. My uncle had arranged for my inheritance to be made available to me in monthly installments, so I had the means to buy a place in Simla, but was that what I wanted? And if I did not want to live in Simla, then where? Monsieur Achilles and I had been in Morocco for a few weeks, and while I'd enjoyed the time there, it had hardly been home, either. London was an option, but with the knowledge that my dear cousins were not living there, the prospect seemed cold indeed. Really, my reasonings aside, New York seemed the most likely place for me to settle.

If for no other reason than that scarcely anyone there would know me as Rose Beckingham, and Nellie Dennet had hardly been notable enough for anyone aside from those closest to me in my old life to recognize me. I could become an unknown and start over should I wish.

I leaned back in the desk chair and stared through the window at the trees lining the path that wrapped around the Hutchins' rented property. I'd taken a walk there that very morning to enjoy the fresh air and contemplate what my day would hold, and I never would have imagined it would hold such a momentous decision. For I felt quite confident I knew what I needed to do.

Standing up from the desk, I tucked the letter in the drawer and then turned for the door. I needed to inform Mrs. Hutchins at once.

≈

IN THE TIME it took me to read Catherine's letter and come to my decision, Mrs. Hutchins had left the library for what seemed the first time in days and gone downstairs. Mr. Hutchins' office door was ajar as I passed it, as well, leading me to believe he would be with his mother. Good, I thought. Better to deliver the news at once. It would save me time.

As I walked down the front stairs and stepped into the entrance hall, however, I heard a third voice coming from the sitting room. A male voice.

"Do not apologize for an unplanned visit," Mrs. Hutchins said, her voice high-pitched in the way it always was when she was speaking to guests. "This house has become as much yours as ours in the past weeks."

"My mother speaks true," Mr. Hutchins said. "You are welcome here anytime, Lieutenant."

"You both are too kind," the third voice said. The voice I now recognized.

I froze in the hallway. Lieutenant Collins was in the sitting room, and suddenly I wanted to sneak back upstairs.

Graham and I had grown close over my short time back in Simla. He had accompanied me on several outings, assisted me in uncovering important information, and had been present for the final part of my fight with Mr. Barlow. And despite me once believing him to be one of the assassins hired by the American, I now understood his remaining close to me stemmed from affection rather than violent intent.

And it was for that very reason I wanted to hide. Mrs.

Hutchins would be upset at the news of my departure from India, but Graham would likely be devastated.

"Let me send a servant to fetch Miss Beckingham for you, Lieutenant," Mrs. Hutchins said, clearing her throat to call out for Jalini or any nearby servant.

"Please, Mrs. Hutchins, you may call me Graham," he said. "And I do not wish to disturb Miss Beckingham if she is busy."

"Surely she was the purpose of your visit, was she not?" Arthur Hutchins asked.

"Arthur," hissed his mother. "Do not embarrass the man. And Graham, I know Rose is as smitten with you as we are. She would hate to know you were here and she missed your company. I'll send for her."

There would be no avoiding the meeting unless I ran out the front door, but even then, there was a chance they would see me from the window. So, I walked through the sitting room door. "No need to send for me. I am here."

The others in the room turned, and I wanted to flush at the color in Graham's cheeks, the light in his eyes at the sight of me.

"I heard you talking from the stairs," I said, perching on the cushion furthest from where Graham sat near the fireplace. "To what do we owe the visit, Lieutenant?"

"Graham," he corrected softly. "And I was simply in the area and thought I would enjoy your company. I hope I'm not intruding."

The Hutchins' bungalow was nowhere near Graham's quarters or anyplace of interest, but I did not point this out and discredit his version of events.

"Of course not," Mrs. Hutchins said, once again reassuring him. "Nothing of note has happened here, so we are glad for your company."

"Actually," Mr. Hutchins added, "I was in the middle of a letter, and while I don't wish to be rude, I think it would be wise for me to finish it while the thought is fresh."

"Arthur," Mrs. Hutchins chastised again, aghast.

"He is not here to see the likes of me," he said. "Or you, for that matter. You should leave the young people alone to discuss things."

Graham looked down at his hands folded in his lap, his cheeks a burning red. My own felt quite hot, but I interrupted Mr. Hutchins in the middle of rising from his spot in the armchair.

"Actually, I wish to speak to all of you," I said, deciding not to delay the announcement. It would be best to tell Graham in front of Mr. and Mrs. Hutchins so he could not argue with me about the decision. My mind would not be changed no matter what he said, so it would be best to avoid it altogether.

Mr. Hutchins sank down in his chair, annoyed, but Mrs. Hutchins and Graham sat up, alert.

"What is it, dear?" Mrs. Hutchins asked.

"She is going to tell us," Arthur sighed.

Mrs. Hutchins shot her son a dirty look, and then gave me an encouraging smile.

I avoided Graham's eyes and began. "I am so grateful to the two of you for offering me a place to stay and welcoming me into your family. It will be very difficult to ever pay you back for the kindness you have bestowed."

"It was our pleasure, dear," Mrs. Hutchins said.

"Besides, without you, we may have never learned the true motivations of the vile Mr. Barlow. Our meeting was destined, and whatever debt you feel you owe has been paid in full, I assure you."

"You are too kind." I tipped my head to her, and she beamed with pride. "And that is precisely the reason it is so hard to announce that I will be leaving your company and Simla."

In the corner of my vision, Graham went rigid. Arthur remained unfazed but Mrs. Hutchins gasped. "Oh dear, that is dreadful news. Are you leaving under happy circumstances?"

With Catherine's letter still a mystery to me, I wasn't entirely certain what I would find upon arriving in New York. But no one needed to know that, anyway. "Yes, in fact. My cousin Catherine has become engaged and wishes for me to come to New York to assist with the wedding preparations."

"Your cousin?" Mrs. Hutchins asked. "Well, if she's as pretty as you are, it was only a matter of time before she settled down. Is he a good man?"

"That is what I hope to find out," I said. "Catherine wants me to meet her beloved, and I have to admit, though this time with you all has been lovely, I do miss my family."

"Of course, you do," she said. "When do you leave?"

"As soon as possible. I will leave for Bombay once my things are packed and transport can be arranged, and then I will board the next ship for America."

Mrs. Hutchins pursed her lips. "We will miss you terribly, but you seem happy to be reunited with your family, and that is all anyone who cares about you could want."

I chanced a look at Graham, who had become suddenly very fascinated with the cold fireplace.

"I am happy," I said. "Though, I am sad to leave you all."

"I will try to arrange a parting dinner before you leave," Mrs. Hutchins said. "I'll talk to the servants at once. Lieutenant Collins, you will clearly be invited as one of Miss Beckingham's closest friends in the city. Will you be free the next several evenings? I don't know if there is time for a formal invitation to be drafted, but—"

Graham stood up quickly, his knee knocking the table in the center of the room and scooting it forward several inches. He bent down to right it and then stood tall. "I just recalled an important meeting I have today. I wish I could stay longer, but I'm afraid I have to leave immediately."

"Oh," Mrs. Hutchins said, standing up. "Well, let us show you out."

"No, please," Graham said, refusing to look at me. "Stay. I can see myself out."

He bowed to the room and stumbled into the hallway like there was fire nipping at his heels. When the front door opened and then slammed closed, Mrs. Hutchins leaned back in her chair and shook her head.

"Oh my," she mused to herself, though loud enough for the room to hear. "The poor man is even more in love with her than I thought."

2

Mrs. Hutchins arranged for a hearty meal that very night as a train was leaving from the hill station the following day, and I intended to be on it.

"Very rushed," she kept mumbling as she ordered the servants around. "No one will be free at such short notice. Just the three of us."

The thought of such a small gathering seemed to vex her, but I found it perfectly suitable. The only other person I would have liked to say goodbye to was Graham, but he seemed uninterested in a goodbye, and I didn't want to bruise his feelings any more than I clearly already had. So, I had my final dinner in Simla with Mrs. Hutchins and her son, who argued the entire meal about various things I hardly paid attention to.

Though I appreciated the effort, I was distracted with thoughts of travel and being in New York again. It had been so many years since I'd been in the city, and I was anxious to be reunited with it as much as with my cousins. Though, there was trepidation, as well, in regards to both.

~

"DID YOU HAVE A FILLING BREAKFAST?" Mrs. Hutchins asked me the next morning. "The food on the trains is barely passable, and I'd hate to send you away wanting."

"It was delicious," I assured her. "And I do not eat much while travelling."

She wrapped her hand around my upper arm. "That explains the thinness. You travel too often for a young, single woman. Will you settle in New York?"

I grabbed my suitcase and held it in front of my legs. If I didn't leave soon, Mrs. Hutchins would keep me talking forever. "I enjoy travelling, so I don't have any thoughts of settling anywhere yet, but I'll be sure to write to you from wherever I do settle."

"That was never a question," she said. "Of course, you'll write. And I'll write to you. We must stay in touch."

"Absolutely," I agreed. "But I'm afraid I really should be going. I want to get to the station early and you know it's no short trip."

Mrs. Hutchins hugged me once more and then instructed Jalini to open the door for me, and as soon as the door opened, I knew my hopes to get to the station early were thoroughly dashed as Graham was walking up the path towards the house.

"Lieutenant!" Mrs. Hutchins called, waving as if the man wasn't already headed our direction. Then, she turned to me, eyes wide. "Do you see what he is carrying?"

Indeed, I had. A suitcase.

"What do you think he is doing with that?" she asked, growing more anxious with every passing second.

"We should wait and let him explain."

Surprisingly, Mrs. Hutchins nodded and allowed Graham to mount the stairs and bow to us both before pouncing on him.

"Travelling somewhere, Lieutenant?"

For the first time since I'd made my announcement, he looked at me, a shy smile on his lips. "I believe that depends on Miss Beckingham."

"Me?" I asked naively, feigning I had no idea what he meant.

He nodded. "If you'll have me, I'd love to accompany you to New York."

I'd expected the proposal, and yet it left me speech-less. I had no idea how to respond.

"That is a long trip," I said. "Do you have business in New York? And will the army permit you to leave on such sudden notice?"

His smile slipped. "I have had more than my share of business lately. And I was due some leave, so was able to pull a few strings. I've always wanted to travel to America."

"It would be a pleasure trip, then?"

"Yes," he said, head bobbing. "Though, I have to admit you are part of my motivation, Miss Beckingham. I would not rest well knowing you were travelling such a long way alone."

I had a suspicion Graham was still not being fully honest with me. "I have travelled unaccompanied many times, Lieutenant. I'd hate for you to go so far out of your way due to unnecessary worry."

"Graham," he corrected again. "I have seen firsthand exactly how capable you are of taking care of yourself, but those memories do not ease the worry that has settled into my heart and mind. Though, I will not go with you if you do not wish me to."

"I don't see why Rose wouldn't want you to join her," Mrs. Hutchins said, stepping forward and laying a hand on my shoulder. "You two have become very close these last few weeks."

True, we had. But part of the reason I had revealed so much of myself to Lieutenant Collins was because I believed I would leave Simla soon and never see him again. Did I want to continue our friendship across oceans? Or risk that friendship blossoming into something more?

Graham looked at me, his thin blond mustache twitching into a nervous smile. "Well, Miss Rose? Do you yet have a verdict? Should I walk this suitcase back to my quarters and unpack or are we off on a transatlantic adventure?"

There was so much hope in his eyes, so much excitement, dampened only by the possibility that I would refuse him. But his feelings could not factor into my decision. Upon arriving in New York, I would have to tend to my cousins, and perhaps help Catherine uncover some truth about her betrothed. I had business and secrets in New York City that Graham didn't expect and might not be able to be privy to. And yet, he had been helpful to me in Simla on more than one occasion. Perhaps, even though he had never been in the city, he could be helpful again.

"Seeing as you are already packed, I don't see how I can say no," I said with a smile.

He all but leapt with excitement, his grin splitting his face.

"The car is leaving now, so you don't have much time to regret your decision and back out," I said.

Graham grabbed my suitcase out of my hands, his fingers brushing slowly across my knuckles as he did, and then walked down the stairs to load our luggage into the car. "Now, why ever would I regret my decision?"

I hugged Mrs. Hutchins once more and followed after Graham, hoping he would never find out the many answers there were to that question. And also that I wouldn't come to regret my own decisions.

He held open the car door, offering me a hand as he helped me inside. When he slid into the seat beside me, he looked like a child on Christmas morning. "Do you think New York City is ready for the likes of us?"

3

The air smelled like spring. I could smell it even over the salt of the ocean, the musty dampness of the ship. I would recognize the smell of New York City—my city—anywhere. I hadn't set foot on its shores for ten years, but seeing the shape of the city against the horizon felt like home. It felt like seeing my mother's face, like walking into the warm embrace of my father as a small girl. It was all I could do not to cry.

"Not as big as I thought," Graham mused next to me.

I wanted to tell him that he would see once he walked the streets, once he moved through the neighborhoods. He would feel the immensity of it. Unlike in Simla, he would be an unknown in the city. Lieutenant Graham Collins would be a nobody.

But I couldn't, of course. Rose Beckingham had never been to America. She'd travelled through Europe and Africa and India, but this would be her first trip to North America.

"Nothing is big compared to the ocean," I said. "I bet

the city will meet all your wildest fantasies once we reach shore.'

The look Graham gave me, his blonde brow lifted, lips fighting a rising smirk, made me blush. I didn't want to know or discuss any more about his fantasies.

Getting off the ship was a mad dash of holding my skirts close so I wouldn't be trampled waiting to go down the gangplank, finding our luggage, and searching for the driver I knew Catherine would have sent. I had managed a quick telegram before my departure, telling Catherine I heartily accepted her invitation and would be leaving on the next ship. I'd heard nothing back from her but I knew my cousin well enough to know she would have tracked my ship, known the expected arrival date, and been prepared to welcome me the way polite society dictated.

Graham walked over with his trunk rolling behind him, dodging and weaving around weary travelers eager to find their rest now that they'd reached their destination. "There is a good hotel a couple of streets down according to the porter."

"If there is a room left," I said, eying the steady stream of ship passengers nervously. "I can speak to my cousin about a room for you. I just forgot to warn them of your accompanying me. I'd hate to offer you a room that may not exist."

And truthfully, after spending so much time together aboard the ship, I was ready to be rid of the Lieutenant for a stretch. He had been a nice travelling companion, if a bit too cautious. Out of a mistrust of everyone else on the ship, he hardly let me out of his sight except to sleep. And even then, I often imagined I could feel him listening outside my door so oppressive was his watchful gaze.

"I would hate to impose when you are reuniting with your family," Graham said. "Besides, a male in the midst of so much female emotion would require a break from it all. It will be nice to have my own room at a hotel."

"Female emotion?" I teased, eyes narrowed. "You make it sound like a poisonous gas."

Graham laughed. "I hope I did not offend you. Mostly, I mean to stay out of the way of you and your family as you reunite."

"That is kind of you," I said.

He readjusted his trunk in his hand and looked around. "Do you see your family or the car nearby?"

"Not yet, but I'm sure it will become easier as the crowd thins," I said. Graham nodded and dropped his trunk. I gestured for him to pick it up. "You do not have to stay."

"Of course, I do. I cannot leave a beautiful woman alone so near the docks."

"I am hardly alone," I said, motioning to the swarm of people.

"Being surrounded by strangers does not make one any less alone," he said.

I knew I would never be rid of him with argument alone, so I lied.

I stretched onto my tiptoes, looking over the crowd, and then gasped. "I do believe I see my cousin moving through the crowd."

"Where is she? I can wave her down."

"She has not seen me yet. And if you wish to avoid an

outburst of female emotion, it would be best if you left now," I said. "Tears will be shed during our reunion, I am sure."

Graham twisted his mouth to the side. "You are certain it is her?"

"As certain as I am that there will be no room for you at the hotel if you do not beat this crowd." I touched his arm gently, giving him a little push. "Please, secure yourself a place to stay and we will rejoin one another later. I slipped the address of my cousins' aunt in your coat pocket."

Graham frowned and reached into his pocket, smiling when he retrieved the note. "A man should watch his wallet around you, Rose Beckingham. I didn't even feel you do this."

He seemed genuinely impressed and surprised at my skills, perhaps most surprised at the fact that I was able to bypass his notice. But he gripped the address in his fingers as he waved goodbye, pulling the trunk behind him as he went.

The strangest part of being Rose Beckingham had been the constant attention. As Nellie Dennet, I went unnoticed all of the time. No one watched me walk down the street or sought out my company at parties. I was the help. A servant of sorts, unimportant in every way. But now, men the likes of Lieutenant Collins worried for my safety and fussed over me.

Achilles Prideaux did not fuss over me, though. Not in the same way, at least. He worried for my safety when I took undue risks during an investigation, but he did not stop me from investigating. He did not worry whether I could handle myself with strangers with bad intentions.

I wondered what Achilles had been doing since we parted. Had he found himself a new partner? A travel companion with innate skills and a pretty face? I couldn't say why, but the thought twisted like a knife in my stomach.

Luckily, I didn't have long to think about it because as it turned out, the lie I'd told Graham hadn't been a lie at all. Catherine and Alice broke through a parting in the crowd and rushed for me before I could fully understand what I was seeing.

"Rose," Alice cried, running for me and throwing her long, thin arms around my waist.

I returned the hug even though I hardly recognized the girl I was holding. "You cut your hair."

It was the only thing I could think to say. Her long brunette hair had been lopped short, finger curls framing her angular face. The last I saw her, she had the roundness of youth in her cheeks. Now, she looked like a woman.

"Catherine convinced me," she said, stepping away and running a nervous hand along her hair. She had traded in the poofy dresses of childhood for a boxy drop-waist silk dress that swayed around her in ripples of luxury, drawing passing eyes. Her lips were rouged, which I knew her father would detest, and her cheeks were washed in a vibrant blush. She looked like her mother. And Rose. The real Rose.

"We are single women in one of the greatest cities in the world," Catherine said, stepping forward, arms open wide for a hug. "We both needed to look the part."

I hugged her, pressing my face into her neck and smiling at Alice over her shoulder. Seeing them felt better than I had imagined. When I pulled away, I held Catherine at arm's length. She looked as she always had, slim and elegant in an olive-green taffeta dress and black t-strap heels, her beaded purse clutched in her manicured hands like she was afraid someone would try to snatch it.

"London is the greatest city in the world," Alice corrected with a frown. "But New York City is a close second."

"Either way, you both look wonderful," I said. "Like you belong here."

"They have acclimated wonderfully to the city," a third voice said. I spun in surprise and then saw the woman who had to be their Aunt Sarah. She looked exactly like Lady Ashton. She stepped forward and extended her hand. "I am their Aunt Sarah, and I'd love to be yours, as well."

She was a petite woman, barely taller than a child, but she had a kind, warm smile, and I felt instantly at ease. I bypassed her outstretched hand and pulled her into a hug. "It is so wonderful to meet you."

She returned the hug without hesitation. "I heard we would have met sooner, but you had business to take care of in Africa? And then Asia, correct? Busy woman."

"Yes, I was sorry to change my plans at the last minute," I said simply.

Catherine smiled from behind her aunt and tipped

her head so subtly it was hardly noticeable. Clearly her letter had been true. She had finally forgiven me for abandoning them in lieu of exploring the world with Monsieur Prideaux.

"But I am thrilled to be here now. Catherine and Alice know the city and can take me to all the best places."

Alice's eyes lit up. "I can, at least. Catherine has become quite boring now that she is engaged."

I startled, turning to my cousin. "I almost forgot. You are going to be married."

Her cheeks warmed and her lips pursed together in a tight smile.

"Is he here?" I asked, looking around in case another member of the party was waiting to step into the fold.

"No," Catherine said, wrapping her arm through mine and pulling me into the crowd. I looked back for my luggage, but a man with a thick mustache and a black hat who I assumed was the driver was taking care of it. "Charles did not want to interrupt our family reunion. He said he would rather meet you at the house when you were less overwhelmed."

"How thoughtful of him," I said.

Catherine nodded, but her smile dimmed. I was eager to pull her aside and speak to her privately about the notes of urgency I picked up on in her letter. But now was not the time.

"Speaking of the man in your life," I said. "I arrived today with a companion, who—"

Alice gasped and practically screamed. "Are you engaged to the French detective? Your letter explained that you went away with him."

I jumped and hoped I did not look nearly as embarrassed as I felt. "No, unfortunately Monsieur Prideaux and I parted ways in Morocco. I have not spoken to him since."

I heard Alice's disappointed sigh behind me, but carried on.

"However, I brought along a *friend* from Simla. His name is Lieutenant Graham Collins. We met only a few weeks ago, but he wished to see New York and asked if he could escort me. I saw no reason to refuse him, so he is in the city, as well."

"Friend?" Catherine asked, eyeing me for any hint of deception.

"Precisely," I answered without hesitation. Though Catherine and Alice still shared a look I knew well.

"Where is he?" Alice asked, running ahead of us, her eyes wide and eager. It was nice to know that not everything about her had changed.

"He is getting settled at his hotel, the reason for his absence similar to that of Charles. He did not wish to intrude on our reunion."

Based on Alice's pouty lower lip, however, Graham would have been a very welcome addition to our party.

"I look forward to meeting him," Aunt Sarah said. Then, she pointed to the nicest car parked along the curb. The sides were cherry red, the top a rich black that seemed to glimmer in the sunlight. "This is mine."

I turned to Catherine and whispered. "Where is Aunt Sarah's husband?"

"Not here, either," she said. "Though, unlike our men, he won't be joining us soon...or ever."

"Oh," I said confused. Then I saw the look in Catherine's face, her eyebrows raised expectantly, and I understood. "*Oh.* He is dead."

She nodded and leaned in, voice low. "I'll explain later."

My luggage was loaded into the car, and then we moved slowly through the streets, avoiding the pedestrians still being purged from the ship.

"How was Africa?" Catherine asked. "Is that where you developed such brown skin or was that in India?"

"A combination of the two, I'm sure." I'd noticed the tanning of my skin only because the powder I used to disguise the scar on my cheek from the bombing had begun to only highlight the injury. It was no longer the same shade as my skin. I hoped time spent in the city would return me to my normal skin tone soon enough. "But it was a very enjoyable trip. More to see than I could ever recount in a single conversation."

And even more that I would never recount. Catherine, and Alice too, I suspected, knew of my interest in mysteries, but they did not need to know how deep that interest ran. They did not need to know that I was in Morocco investigating an international assassin ring. And they did not need to know that I had encountered and killed two such assassins. I could tell by the looks on their faces—and that of their Aunt Sarah's—that I was already seen as an oddity. A woman outside the bounds of normal society. And I did not need to make myself even more of a spectacle by announcing my secret life as a private detective.

Catherine grabbed my hand and twined her fingers

through mine as though we had done it a thousand times before. She patted the back of my hand with her own, highlighting the stark difference between my hand and her alabaster one. "Luckily, we have time for many conversations, cousin. You can tell us all about your adventures."

"And I certainly will," I lied.

4

Aunt Sarah and my cousins pointed out the neighborhoods to me through the window as we passed, but I knew them already. Had walked them many times. Especially the wealthier neighborhoods. My brother and I would escape our family's small apartment to mingle among the old and new money in Washington Square and Madison Square Park. We would wander Fifth Avenue, hungry for the price even a carved banister from their stairs could fetch us.

And now, I would be staying in one of those homes.

As we neared the end of a block, brick and stone mansions rising up around us like castles, one house stood out. It was a corner lot, with two faces open to the public, each more extravagant than the other. The house was constructed with white stone polished to a shine and large, open windows that made me wonder how the house was still standing. Towers and chimneys and decorative parapets rose all over the roof, making it hard to know where to focus. Until we turned the corner and I saw the elaborate gothic arches and spires drawing my eyes upwards to the heavens. The structure was astounding.

Even more astounding, the car parked along the curb in front of the mansion.

"Is this your home?" I asked, my awe obvious.

Aunt Sarah smiled shyly. "Yes. I've always loved making a statement."

I leaned out the window and gazed up, squinting against the sun. "This certainly makes a statement."

Alice leaned in and whispered, "Wait until you see the inside."

Marble as far as the eye could see. Gold detailing on all the trim and columns, murals on the domed ceilings, and lavish velvet and intricately carved wooden furniture filled every room with more riches than any one person could ever possibly take in. I had the feeling I could wander the house for years and still not enjoy every detail in every room.

Had the driver not carried in my luggage and handed it to a servant to take to my room, I would have forgotten it completely. I followed Aunt Sarah through the house while she remarked on the mundane uses of every extraordinary room.

"This is the dining room," she said, pointing to a table as long as the Hutchins' bungalow. "Clearly."

She showed me the kitchens, which had the lowest ceilings and least natural light because they were mostly utilized by the servants, but were still extraordinary. By the time we made it to the sitting room—the fireplace was framed in a border of cut marble that had been lain to look like floral bouquets—I wanted to close my eyes to try and absorb what I'd already seen before taking in any more.

The guest rooms were, thankfully, less opulent. The fabrics hanging from the four-poster beds were lush and many of the fine detailings from the rest of the house were repeated for the sake of continuity, but I felt comfortable in these rooms. One of them would be a fine place to call home for awhile.

Seeing the luxury around me, I almost felt guilty for pushing Graham into a hotel room. He could have stayed in a guest room on the opposite side of the mansion, and we never would have run into one another.

Aunt Sarah showed me to the end of a hall and pushed open a heavy wooden door. "This will be your room for as long as you are staying here. Which, you should know, may be as long as you like."

"Thank you for your kindness," I said. "I can see already you are a very generous host."

She tucked her hands in front of her simple blue dress that hung slightly too long on her small frame. She hardly looked like a woman who would be the owner of a home so grand. "These halls have been quiet too long. Having Catherine and Alice these last few months has been a delight. And the way they talk about you, I know we will all become a very happy family, indeed."

"Indeed," I agreed.

She beamed at me, and then shook her head like she'd just remembered something. "Now, I ought to let you get settled. You are no doubt weary from travel. Dinner will be served at seven, but my kitchen is open to you anytime. Please, make yourself at home here. Whatever is mine, is yours, dear Rose."

After Aunt Sarah left, I finished pulling out the few items in the bottom of the trunk the servants had left alone—letters from the Ashtons, my cousins, and Achilles; a photo of a young Rose with her parents that had been given to me by Lady Ashton when she realized very little of Rose's personal belongings had been delivered to me; and the golden locket I had carried with me since leaving New York.

I'd worn it for years, never taking it off because of its connection to my old life. To New York, my parents, my brother. Although my promise to find my brother was now settled, being back in this city again stirred up old memories. I found myself reaching into the bottom of the trunk and pulling the locket over my head. It settled against my chest, and I had just tucked it beneath the collar of my dress when there was a light knock on my bedroom door. Before I could go to open it, the door opened and Catherine stepped inside.

"Sorry to intrude," she said, not looking sorry in the least.

I was about to tease her on the matter when I noted her face. The warm smile she'd greeted me with at the dock was gone. She wore a weary expression, lines forming around her eyes and mouth that I couldn't believe I didn't notice sooner.

She seemed so happy at the docks, as fierce and vibrant as ever, that I had almost begun to doubt whether anything was wrong at all. I wondered if I hadn't imagined a problem as an excuse to come back to New York City. But the moment she pushed the door shut behind her and turned to face me, I knew I'd been correct. Something was wrong.

"What is it, cousin?" I asked.

"It has been months since we've seen one another. Is it not allowed for me to want to be near you?"

"It is allowed," I said with a smile. *Though unusual.* Catherine had always seemed content to keep her distance. From me and even her friends and family. She was not silly or flirtatious or a gossip. But she had an iron will and a scathing glare she had no qualms about using. It made her intimidating. My guess had always been that she preferred to be alone and people preferred to steer clear of her wrath.

But I couldn't imagine this Catherine intimidating anyone. She looked exhausted.

"So, you must tell me about your betrothed," I said, deciding directness would be the best strategy. "Your letter teased of the story of your meeting, but I was denied the details."

She sighed like it cost her to retell the story, but then began to recite the details as if reading from a script. "We were at the embassy for one reason or another regarding our stay in New York when a group of men in suits came through the front doors. Alice, of course, paid fierce attention to them, and while I was teasing her about being a shameless flirt, one of the men stepped forward from the group and introduced himself."

"Your Charles?" I asked.

She nodded, a light flickering in her eyes. "Yes, my Charles. He told me instantly that I was the most beautiful woman he'd ever seen, and he would rather die than never see me again."

"Quite the romantic," I said.

Catherine's smile grew slightly warmer, her cheeks coloring. "You haven't the faintest idea, Rose. He is always complimenting me and doting on me. Even Alice, the most romantic person either of us knows, finds our courtship nauseating."

"So, it was love at first sight?"

"It was," Catherine said, and the light that seemed to shine out of her eclipsed all the opulent decorations in the room. She was radiant when talking about her fiancé. So, I couldn't imagine what the issue could be.

"You must be excited to introduce him to your parents, then," I said. "And will the wedding be held in London or at the family estate in Somerset? You could make either lovely, but the Somerset foliage in the fall would be heavenly. You'd hardly have need of decorations."

Catherine seemed to sag where she stood to the point I worried she would tip over. "I haven't thought much about the wedding, if I'm being quite honest."

I frowned. "That seems unlike you."

"Yes," she agreed, looking down at the floor.

I crossed the room to wrap an arm around her waist and led her to the tufted chairs in front of the fireplace where we both sat facing one another. To further prove she was not behaving as herself, she did not fight me once. I reached out and took her hands in mine. "Please tell me what is wrong."

"Can you tell so easily?" she asked. "No one else has seemed to notice anything is amiss. Not even Alice. If they have, they are afraid to mention it."

"People are not always as perceptive as we hope them to be. But I wondered if something wasn't wrong when I received your letter."

She smiled at me, and though it seemed to strain her, it looked genuine. "You are just as clever as I hoped, Rose."

I shrugged. "It was simple enough to guess at. When has Catherine Beckingham ever begged anyone for anything? If you were begging me, I knew things had to be dire."

"They are," she said, tucking one ankle under the other and folding her fingers nervously in her lap. "It is about Charles."

"I suspected as much."

She nodded and continued. "He has changed, Rose. In the weeks since we met, he has become a different person."

"Has he become violent?" I asked. "Has he hurt you?"

Her eyes widened in shock. "No, of course not. Never. He dotes on me as he always has."

I sighed in relief. "Then how has he changed?"

Catherine's short blonde hair curled over her ear, and she reached a hand up to tuck it back into place, chewing nervously on her lip. "He has always been a light, happy man. I do not know that I've heard him speak a negative word in all the time we've known one another."

I must have looked just as surprised as I felt because when Catherine looked up at me, her face twisted into disapproval and she reached out and pinched my arm.

I yelped. "Catherine!"

"I know what you were thinking," she said. "Exactly what everyone else has been thinking. *What could a man like Charles Cresswell possibly want with her?*"

"No, in fact," I said, rubbing the sore spot on my arm and trying not to laugh. "I was thinking it was a wonder *you* liked *him*. I always imagined you would meet a man much like yourself."

"And what would a man like that be like?" she asked, trying to entrap me.

"Beautiful and charming," I said, winking at her.

Catherine rolled her eyes, looking hardly convinced, and leaned back in her chair to continue. "In any case, his demeanor has changed. He is withdrawn, speaking very little of his day-to-day, and has become secretive. He rarely tells me where he is going or when he will be back. We do not go out together as often as we once did. He favors staying indoors, and is hesitant to meet new people."

"It is not uncommon for people to change once they are in a relationship," I said, though I had no such experience. Working for the Beckinghams in India had kept me busy, and my time since had been filled with mystery and murder to the point that a suitor would have been a dangerous distraction. Still, I could guess at his motivations. "Perhaps, he now favors spending time alone with you rather than going out."

"Perhaps," Catherine allowed. "Though that would not explain the secretiveness."

"No, it wouldn't. Do you have any idea what could be causing this?"

"I am not the one who spent time with a world-renowned detective," she snapped. Then, she shook her head. "Forgive me. I do have a thought. It's just not a very nice one."

I reached out and touched her folded hands gently. "Our conversation will not leave this room. You can be candid."

Catherine bit her lower lip, which looked ragged from her nervous chewing, and loosed a shaky exhale. "I don't want to believe it, but it is possible he has changed his mind about marrying me and is just too kind to say so."

I shook my head instantly. "A truly kind man would never play with your heart in such a cruel way. If that is the reason for his sudden change in behavior, then he has never been kind and you are better without him."

Catherine managed a weak smile. "It is just that nothing else seems to explain the circumstances as thoroughly as that. And whether he is unkind or not, I still love him." She turned her face away from me, and I could see tears welling in her eyes. "Deeply."

Seeing Catherine so vulnerable was rare, and I knew she was opening up to me in a way she hadn't to anyone else. She was allowing me into her world, and I did not want to ruin it. So, I spanned the distance between us and laid a hand on her shoulder. "I am sorry."

My words seemed to bring her back to herself, and she sat up straighter, pointed chin jutting out. "I did not bring you here to be a sympathetic ear. I have plenty of those around should I require one."

I pulled my hand back. "Oh? Why did you bring me here, then?"

"Are we going to pretend you haven't solved murders, one of which was committed by my brother and your cousin?" she asked, the glassiness in her eyes gone, replaced with the stoniness I remembered. "Obviously, I brought you here to assist me in uncovering the reason behind his sudden transformation. Even though I have my own theory, I am desperate for it to be wrong, which is why I wrote to you."

"I was never hired to solve those cases," I argued. The only case I'd been formally asked to investigate was an art theft. And I'd accompanied Achilles Prideaux to Morocco, but that had been his case, no matter how much I stuck my nose into the details.

"That does not change the fact that you did," Catherine said. "And if you are willing to assist strangers, how could you refuse your family? Your blood, Rose?"

Once again, Catherine was begging, but this time it was in person. Reading it in writing had been compelling, but seeing the pull of her brows, the woeful downturn of her lips, made it almost impossible to refuse her.

I sighed. "I cannot make any promises, but I will do my best to uncover...something."

Catherine clapped her hands together as though she'd just completed a tedious chore and then stood up, smoothing down her dress. "That is wonderful to hear, dearest cousin, because Charles is on his way to the house as we speak to meet you. He will be joining us this evening for dinner."

My mouth gaped and too many questions to sort through filled my head, but before I could say anything, Catherine spun on her heel and left the room.

5

Catherine paced in the entryway for the entire hour before Charles arrived for dinner. She was dressed in a beaded gown that cut a clean line down her trim frame, glittering fringe hanging from the bottom. Her hair was glossy and freshly curled with a feathered headband holding it in place. She looked lovely —maybe a touch too lovely for the occasion. And frantic.

Even Alice took notice.

"You're going to wear grooves into the marble," she said, perched in a chair in the sitting room. She was leaning forward to look at her sister around an open French door. "Come sit and talk with me. You will spend the rest of the night with Charles anyway."

"You will understand when you have a suitor of your own," Catherine said.

"I understand now," Alice said. "I am not a child. But until I have a suitor of my own, you should come keep me company."

"Let Rose keep you company. She hasn't even been

here one entire day. You haven't yet wearied her with your constant chatter."

"You've kept her to yourself, as well," Alice grumbled. "You two were gossiping most of the afternoon and no one invited me. Just because I do not travel the world with different men or have a fiancé doesn't mean I don't have anything interesting to say. You'd be surprised what I overhear."

Catherine went rigid, spinning around and filling the doorway into the sitting room. I could only see a sliver of Alice in the space between the sleeve of Catherine's dress and her side. Her eyes were wide, but there was a kind of excitement in them.

"What did you hear?" Catherine asked.

"Lots of things," Alice said. "People pay me little notice, so I do a good bit of eavesdropping. I bet you'd love to know what the servants think of you."

Catherine shook her head. "I don't care about the servants. I mean today. You said you saw us in Rose's room. What did you hear?"

Alice's smug expression turned curious. "Nothing. Why?" She leaned forward, head turned to one side like she expected Catherine to whisper a secret in her ear. "Was there something to hear?"

Catherine stared at her sister for a moment, and I sat on the stairs with no desire to come between them. When she was confident Alice didn't know anything, Catherine returned to pacing the entry hall.

Alice jumped up from her chair and stood in the doorway, hands resting on her narrow hips. Even with her short haircut and new clothes, she looked like a child.

"What were you two talking about? If there is something going on, I have every right to know. I'm sixteen, not six."

"Then stop acting like it," Catherine spat just as a knock sounded on the door. Her deep frown flipped in an instant. She stood tall and almost ran to the door, beating out a servant who was making their way to answer it.

"That will be Charles," Alice said, rolling her eyes.

I stood up and smoothed down my dress. It was freshly ironed and completely without wrinkle, but I still fussed with the mauve chiffon.

Since promising Catherine I would do my best to uncover the reason for the behavior change in her love, I couldn't push the thought from my mind that maybe she was right. Maybe her theory that he simply no longer wished to marry her would prove true, and I would have to deliver that news to her. It would break her heart.

Catherine presented an unflappable front, but I had seen a hint of the softness she kept hidden. And if I told her Charles no longer loved her, I felt she would crumble apart. She so clearly loved him and was desperately worried about him, and I wanted nothing more than for her theory to be wrong. And the moment Catherine pulled open the door and I saw the way Charles looked at her, I knew that it was.

Charles looked at Catherine from head to toe, and love seemed to pour off of him like water spilling from an already full glass. There was nowhere for it to go, so it filled the room. Standing on either side of the doorway looking at one another, they practically glowed.

Alice sighed and walked back into the sitting room.

"You are a picture," Charles said, grabbing Catherine's hand and pressing it to his lips. When he dipped low, he had a small bald spot at the center of his head, and when he stood again, I noticed the speckles of gray hair at his temples. When Catherine clutched his fingers and pulled him into the entry way, I noticed the deep creases in his forehead and around his mouth.

I hadn't thought to ask Catherine how old her beloved was. I'd assumed they were similar in age, but Charles looked like he could be a peer of her father, Lord Beckingham. Though, there was something more vivacious about him. His face was square and handsome, and he looked like someone more than capable of handling Catherine.

"Sorry I am late," he said, standing close to my cousin, his eyes drinking in her face. "I hope you have not been waiting."

"No, not at all," Catherine said. "We are still waiting on Aunt Sarah before we are ready to leave."

I heard Alice mutter something about her sister lying from the other room, but if Charles heard it, he paid it no mind.

"I have been busy catching up with my cousin." Catherine turned and extended a hand to me. I took it and she pulled me close, tucking her arm affectionately around my waist. "Rose, this is Charles Cresswell. Charles, this is Rose Beckingham."

Charles Cresswell's eyes widened like he was surprised someone else had been in the room the entire time, and it was no wonder. He didn't seem to have eyes for anyone but Catherine.

He grabbed my hand and bowed low. "Pleased to

meet you, Miss Beckingham. Katie has told me so much about you."

"Katie?"

Catherine chuckled and batted at Charles' chest. "A pet name. I have already warned Alice that if she takes to calling me that, I'll never speak to her again."

Charles pressed his cheek to the top of her head. "I will stop if you don't like it."

She turned and smiled up at him. "Don't you dare. I like it when you say it."

They were looking at one another in a way that, to be fair to Alice, was making my stomach feel a little uneasy, when another knock resounded through the entrance hall.

Suddenly, Aunt Sarah rushed into the room, opening her arms when she saw Charles. "Mr. Cresswell. I thought that would be you. So good to see you."

"Actually, that wasn't me," he said, turning to the door. "Not sure who it is. Would you like me to answer it for you?"

"No, absolutely not. You are my guest." She turned and called over her shoulder for a servant just as a small brunette woman with wide eyes and pale lips walked into the room. The girl went immediately to the door and pulled it open, stepping aside to reveal Lieutenant Graham Collins standing on the top stair.

He had on his military finest, his hat tucked beneath his arm, and was standing tall. His blonde hair shone gold in the early evening light, and his mustache twitched into a smile when he saw me.

Aunt Sarah frowned. "Hello. How may I help you?"

Graham opened his mouth to respond, but was cut off by Alice, who had decided the gathering was now worthy of her time. She pushed past her sister and Charles, who were already whispering to one another, ignoring the stranger at the door, and tipped her head to Graham.

"Welcome. I am Alice. What is your name?" She had on the most mischievous smile I'd ever seen, and even Graham seemed embarrassed by the full force of her attention.

Before things could get out of hand, I stepped forward. "This is my friend, Lieutenant Graham Collins. He came with me all the way from India to ensure I travelled safely."

"How chivalrous," Alice crooned.

"So happy to have you, Lieutenant," Aunt Sarah said. "Will you be joining us for dinner? We are just leaving for the restaurant."

Graham's eyebrows went up as he looked to me for the answer. "Well, I'm not sure. I just came to make sure Rose had settled in all right. She gave me the address, and I worry I may have abused it by coming at dinner time."

"There can never be too many friendly faces around the dinner table," Aunt Sarah said. "Especially when one is a weary traveler who has taken such good care of one of my nieces."

It didn't seem to matter to Sarah that I was not related to her in the slightest, and I appreciated her warm and speedy welcome into the family.

"Besides," she added, "a handsome young man with an accent should not be out on the town alone. Single women will swarm and overwhelm him. A strapping man like you will need to be seen with a woman on your arm if you hope to keep your uniform so nice and pressed."

"Is that so?" Graham asked, his eyes darting to me to gauge what I thought of that idea.

I tried to keep my face neutral. "You have arrived at the perfect time for dinner, and I know my cousins have been anxious to meet my travel companion."

Alice stepped forward, smiling so wide I thought it must have hurt, but Catherine managed little more than a small nod before she was once again whispering with Charles. If things continued as they were, there wouldn't be time for me to speak with Charles alone and solve anything.

Graham stepped inside just as the driver appeared in the doorway, announcing the car was ready. Charles escorted Catherine on one side and Aunt Sarah on the other, and when Graham provided an arm for me to grab, it was snatched away by an eager Alice. Graham, ever the gentleman, turned and offered me his other arm, and we were off. One big happy family.

6

Aunt Sarah seemed to know everyone as we moved through the dimly-lit restaurant. She talked with women from her garden society and church. And based on small snippets of conversation I was able to overhear, she even seemed to be part of several women's clubs that had been devoted to women's suffrage and were now fighting for equal rights. I wondered what Lord Ashton thought of his wife's politically-minded sister.

The host at the restaurant seemed to like Aunt Sarah best of all, and when she slipped the man a large bill for showing us to our reserved table, I understood why. I reminded myself to ask Catherine later how Sarah had come to command such a large fortune.

"Almost as nice as the White Tiger Club in Simla," Graham whispered in my ear.

For a moment, I thought he was serious, until I looked into his face. His eyes were wide at the crystal chandeliers hanging from the ceiling in even measure and the mirrored walls reflecting the tables so the room seemed to go on forever in every direction. Everyone wore their finest, and I wished I'd selected something nicer.

Once we were seated, Aunt Sarah ordered for the table without asking, and no one, not even the men, seemed to mind. I was simply glad for one less thing to worry about, and I folded up my menu happily.

"So, Rose," Charles said, leaning around Catherine to smile at me. With his full attention on me finally, it was easy to see how Catherine could have softened to his charms. Even with the age difference, a younger version of Charles lived in his smile. "Catherine tells me you spent time in Morocco."

"Yes. Only a few weeks, unfortunately. Have you ever been?"

"Never," he said. "Though I've always wanted to."

"You absolutely should." It was shocking how much I sounded like a born and raised daughter of fortune. No one would guess based on this conversation that I had grown up in one of the worst neighborhoods of this very city. Sometimes, even I could forget that part of my past. "Though, perhaps you should go in winter."

He laughed. "Are you not a fan of the heat?"

"I spent many years living in India, and I never quite acclimated."

"You acclimated better than Mrs. Hutchins," Graham said, laughing as though he had just told a riotous joke. The rest of the table smiled uncomfortably, having no idea who Mrs. Hutchins was.

"Mrs. Hutchins gave me a home during my most

recent stay in Simla," I explained. "She was a lovely woman who could not stand the heat. I have no idea why she accompanied her son to India."

Everyone nodded in understanding, but Graham continued our private joke. "Every time I visited the house, she was in the library complaining of the oppressive weather. She would have been happier in the Arctic."

Aunt Sarah laughed and then turned to me. "I hope you will forgive me for saying so, but I was surprised when I heard you had travelled back to Simla so soon. Did you have business there?"

"No forgiveness necessary," I said. "The only business I had there was making my peace with the past."

Catherine grabbed my hand and then held her water glass high. "To making peace."

In a surprising show of affection, Charles leaned over and pressed a kiss to Catherine's temple, brushing his hand down her hair. "If only everyone in the world could be as lovely as my Katie."

"If they were, there would be no end to wars," Alice teased.

Catherine glared at her sister, but Charles just shook his head. "There is much to be said for speaking your mind, which Catherine does quite well. The people I deal with would rather talk with their armies than their words. It makes for very violent resolutions."

"Catherine mentioned you two met at the embassy, Mr. Cresswell. What exactly do you do there?" I asked.

"Nothing worth discussing over dinner," Charles joked. "Mostly paperwork."

"Oh, dear," Catherine said, squeezing Charles' hand.

"Your job is very interesting. Really, Rose, he is always telling me of the important men he meets throughout the day. Many come to him for advice."

"Katie loves me, therefore her opinion cannot be trusted," Charles said. "Everything is interesting to a woman in love."

Catherine wanted to argue, but then she looked into her fiancé's eyes, and the fight seemed to drain out of her. Alice groaned and aggressively unfolded her napkin in her lap.

"What of your responsibilities, Mr. Collins?" Aunt Sarah asked. "Being a Lieutenant must be worthy of discussing over dinner."

"Similar to Mr. Cresswell's job, mine is hardly worth mentioning," Graham said. "I command a platoon of thirty men, but with the war over for so long now paperwork rules the day."

"You all make war sound like a social obligation," Aunt Sarah said. "If I had dealt with the specifics of a war, I don't know that I would ever again talk of anything else. In fact, most of my best stories are from the Great War, and I did not even fight."

"Did you see battle, Mr. Collins?" Alice asked, leaning so far out of her chair I thought the legs would buckle beneath her.

"Graham," he corrected with a smile. "And yes, I did."

"No one wants to discuss war, Alice," Catherine said, chastising her sister.

"I am not forcing him," Alice retorted. "Besides, I want to discuss it."

"That is because you were only a child when it

ended," Catherine said. "The rest of us lived through it and do not wish to again."

Alice opened her mouth to say something, possibly to point out that Catherine herself was also practically a child during the time she referred to, but Aunt Sarah cleared her throat and laughed. "Whether at home or out on the town, sisters will be sisters. How ever did you live with these two for so long in London, Rose? Did they bicker then as they do now?"

"Perhaps the problem has become worse since I last saw them," I said. And in fact, it had. Now that Alice was growing into a woman, it seemed she was not as willing to heed the wisdom of her older sister. "But their many charms outweigh this one fault."

Catherine raised a brow at me, not believing I was being honest for a second, but Charles nodded in robust agreement.

The food came out in a processional, and we all went silent as a spiced baked ham was placed in the center of the table and surrounded by bowls overflowing with fresh salads, speckled with oil and seasonings and bright sticks of vegetables. Brown crusted bread was cracked in half and buttered, and we passed it around the table, each tearing off our own share. When our plates were full, we set to eating, anything beyond the taste of the food before us too distant to pay any mind. And it wasn't until I was full that I began to look around the table and the room again, paying attention to something other than meat and herbs.

The host who had seated us and received the large tip from Aunt Sarah was leading a balding man holding a derby hat through the room, smiling widely and laughing loud enough to be heard over the dull roar of the other diners. I wondered whether he would receive a tip as generous as the one Aunt Sarah had given him. The middle-aged man seemed to be smiling genuinely, and like everyone else in the restaurant, he looked wealthy enough to lose a large bill without noticing.

Then, the host cut around a table and headed towards us. I realized the table next to us, which had belonged to a beautiful young couple who whispered and smiled at one another throughout the entire meal, was now vacant. The man surveyed his dinner mates, perusing the tables around his own, but when his eyes landed on our table, he frowned. He leaned forward, trying to get a better look at someone, and then his eyebrows lifted.

"Charles Cresswell?"

Charles had been cutting Catherine's pork for her, and as soon as he heard his name, he jolted and dropped the fork. It clattered to the floor, and a waiter was at our table with a fresh one in an instant.

"Edward Taylor," he said, rising from his seat to greet the man with a firm handshake. Catherine stood up, as well, taking a position just behind Charles' shoulder. "This is my fiancé, Catherine."

"Lovely to meet you," Edward said, bowing low and kissing Catherine's knuckles.

"How do you two know one another?" Catherine asked.

"Old friends," Edward said, smiling at Charles like he couldn't believe his own eyes. "We have known one another for...ten years. Is that right, Charles? We are getting old."

"Old friends, indeed," Charles agreed with a laugh. "Edward still had his hair when we met."

"And yours was less gray," Edward said, reaching out and brushing Charles' temple affectionately.

Aunt Sarah stood up and walked around the table. "I must meet the man who is willing to tease Charles Cresswell. He is so kind and friendly that no one I've ever met has dared."

Edward shook Aunt Sarah's hand, head tipped back in a laugh. "What does it say about my own character that I am willing? Probably nothing good."

"Nonsense," Charles said, pulling out Catherine's chair for her to sit and then reclaiming his own. "You are a better man than you think, and I am worse than most people think."

"You two appear to know one another well, then?" I asked, unable to pass up the opportunity to speak to a self-described old friend of Charles'. I extended my hand, and Edward leaned around Catherine to accept it. "Rose Beckingham."

Something in Edward's smile faltered, but he regained his composure quickly. "Very well. Friendships forged in war tend to stand the test of time."

"More war talk," Catherine muttered under her breath. Alice beamed, pleased for Catherine to be proven wrong.

"You fought together?" Aunt Sarah asked.

"No," both men said at the same time, turning to one another and smiling when they realized. Edward continued speaking. "I met Charles during the Peace Conference in Paris at the end of the war."

Graham sat up taller. "You were both at the Conference?"

Edward nodded, but Charles took a long drink of his water.

"You never told me that," Catherine said, smiling, though her brows were pulled together in wonder and concern.

Charles smiled, but it didn't reach his eyes. "Nothing to tell, Katie."

"You've been saying that a lot," she whispered, loud enough only for me and Charles to hear.

"I'd say there is a bit to tell." Edward waved away the waiter who had twice now come to try and settle the diner into his seat and bring him a beverage. "He had the ear of one of the most powerful men in the world. Charles here advised the British Prime Minister himself during the talks."

"Really?" Graham asked, mouth hanging open.

Charles smiled and shrugged, but he looked like he wanted to shrink into his suit and disappear.

"Yes," Edward answered since it didn't appear Charles would. "I hardly played a role at all, not even worthy of a footnote, but Charles had a great role."

Catherine was still staring at her betrothed, and Charles patted her knee beneath the table. "Speaking to important men does not make one important. It also does not mean they listened to me."

"They listened to you," Edward said, running a hand through the slicked back bit of hair on the side of his head. "And with Germany rising once again through the ranks, as if to reclaim power, we may need your wisdom sooner than we'd like."

Alice gasped. "War? You think there will be another?"

"I do not expect trouble for many years to come yet, but there are some troubling signs for the future," Edward began.

"Katie was right before," Charles said quickly, pushing his dinner plate away from him and folding his hands in his lap. "War and treaties do not make appropriate dinner conversation. Let us talk of happier things."

"Speaking of happier things," Edward said, bowing. "If I stand for another second, I'll fall over of starvation. It was lovely to meet you all. And Charles, good to see you again. We should meet and catch up when war talk would be more appropriate."

Charles nodded as Edward sat down, and Catherine did her best to shift the conversation away from him and back to Aunt Sarah and her many committees, but it was obvious the mood had changed. Within ten minutes, Charles stood up suddenly, the table rattling where he knocked it with his hip, and cleared his throat.

"You all have been wonderful company, but I'm feeling tired."

"Are you sick, Mr. Cresswell?" Aunt Sarah asked. "My driver can take you home and—"

"No, not sick," he said, smiling politely. "Just tired. I think I will excuse myself and retire for the evening."

"And I will go with him," Catherine said. "Or, rather, I'll go to my own home at the same time."

Alice snickered into her napkin, amused at her sister's verbal stumbling.

Charles tried to argue that it wasn't necessary, but one stern look from Catherine silenced him. Everyone said their goodbyes, and as Catherine turned to leave, she shot a knowing look in my direction.

This was the exact kind of behavior she had been telling me about, and now it was my responsibility to figure out why it was happening.

AUNT SARAH ORDERED tarts and cakes and cookies for the table, along with an assortment of freshly-squeezed juices, but it was difficult to enjoy the delicious food when two of our party were missing.

"I do hope Charles is not ill," Aunt Sarah said, clearly thinking the same thing I was.

"Do you think it could be the food?" Alice asked, looking nervously at the slice of cake in front of her.

Aunt Sarah shook her head. "Never. This restaurant is quite nice. Best chef in the city. It would sooner burst into flames than serve undercooked meat."

"It is more common than you'd think," Graham said. "There were several outbreaks of 'unexplained illness' at the White Tiger Club. Rumors spread of an unclean kitchen despite their efforts to keep it all under wraps."

"The White Tiger Club," Aunt Sarah said, eyes narrowed. "I recognize the name."

"It is popular with British diplomats staying in

Simla," I said. "Perhaps, you've heard someone mention it before."

Aunt Sarah nodded like that could explain it, but then she lifted one finger to alert us to a new idea. "No, I read it recently. A British general died at the White Tiger Club, did he not?"

My throat clenched. If war was unsuitable for dinner conversation, then certainly staged suicides that were actually murders were unfit, as well.

"General Thomas Hughes," Graham said softly, shaking his head. "Terrible tragedy."

"Were they able to uncover who did it?" Aunt Sarah whispered.

"Suicide," Graham said.

I turned to him sharply. He knew the truth just as I did, but when he looked at me, I saw the weariness in his eyes. He had no desire to explain the circumstances, either. It was easier to stick to the official story.

"Absolutely dreadful," Aunt Sarah said.

"Did someone say my name?" Edward was standing next to our table once again, one hand tucked into his pocket.

Aunt Sarah shrieked with laughter, pressing a hand to her chest. "Mr. Taylor. Who ever would refer to you as dreadful?"

"You'd be surprised," he said, winking. Then, he looked around the table and frowned. "Did Charles leave already?"

"He wasn't feeling well," Aunt Sarah said, her lower lip sticking out in sympathy. "But you are still welcome to join us, Mr. Taylor. Your humor would be appreciated here. Miss Beckingham and Mr. Collins only just got off a ship this afternoon, so although lovely, they are exhausted from travel and not up to much conversation."

Edward turned to me. "Where did you come from?"

"Bombay," I explained. "Simla before that."

"Simla," he repeated, brow furrowed.

Edward Taylor did not seem the kind of man to be bothered by a direct line of questioning, so I asked the question as soon as it rose to my mind. "Are you surprised anyone would travel to Simla or do you know my family's history with the city?"

He blinked, and in the corner of my vision, I saw Aunt Sarah's eyes widen and Graham stiffen. "I'm sorry, Miss Beckingham. I hope I have not made you uncomfortable."

"Not in the slightest," I said with a warm smile. "Death is a difficult topic for even the most war-hardened men to discuss."

And true to my statement, Edward gulped audibly. "That is true. It does not help that I knew your father. Quite well, in fact."

I stilled, studying Edward, replaying our interactions in my mind.

He had given me a quizzical look when I'd first announced myself, and I'd assumed it was because he recognized my last name from the papers. But now, I wondered whether he wasn't picturing the real Rose Beckingham in his mind, comparing her face to mine. We looked similar, yes. But there were differences. Subtle and often unnoticed, but to a keen eye, it could be obvious I was an imposter. Especially if Edward Taylor and Mr.

Beckingham were close friends. It would look strange, indeed, if the daughter of his good friend failed to recognize him.

I did my best to remain composed.

"Is that so?" I asked. "I do not recall ever seeing you, but Father had so many friends. He was a very well-liked man."

"He was," Edward agreed. "But do not worry yourself with me. I don't believe we ever had the pleasure of meeting. I knew your father in almost exclusively a business capacity."

"That seems right because Father rarely brought his business home," I said. "Mother didn't like him overworking himself, so 'business is for the office,' she would say."

Edward smiled. "See, it is exactly that kind of thing I would like to know. I have spent the better part of this last year mourning a man I hardly knew. We always talked of spending a holiday together—me and my children and him and his. I always thought we had more time."

I reached out and placed a hand on Edward's suit jacket sleeve, offering him a sympathetic smile. "We all think we have more time until we do not."

He nodded and then his lips pinched together, determined. "Would you want to join me for lunch, Miss Beckingham?"

"Lunch?" I looked over at Aunt Sarah as if for permission. She and Alice were both watching our exchange as if it was a play put on for their entertainment.

"If it isn't any trouble," he added quickly. "I don't know how long you are in the city, but I would love to talk with you more about your father. Perhaps, learning more about him could settle some of the guilt I've felt since his unfortunate end."

Even though Mr. Beckingham was not my actual father, I knew a great deal about him. I lived with him for nine years of my life. I could talk about him over a lunch with an old business partner, especially if that business partner could provide any clues as to why the Beckinghams were targeted by the assassin, Mr. Barlow.

"Yes, absolutely," I said. "My father would want me to do whatever is necessary to ease the mind of an old friend. And I would like to learn more about the kind of work he did."

"I know it is short notice, but would you be free tomorrow?" Edward Taylor grinned down at me, and the look in his eyes made me wonder if he wasn't expecting a similar outcome to the pairing between his peer and my cousin, Catherine.

I opened my mouth to respond, but Graham interrupted, resting his arm on the back of my chair. "Actually, I hoped to inquire about whether you could tour the city with me tomorrow, Rose."

And before I could answer Graham's proposal, Edward stepped away, his smile dimming. "Of course. You are a young woman in a new city. I was a foolish old man to think you'd be free on short notice. I will send word to you soon about setting up a meeting together."

I wanted to refuse Graham and accept Edward's offer, but to do so would be an insult to Graham and perhaps convince Edward that I did have a deeper interest in him than just for information. So, as much as I wanted to do otherwise, I told him that would be wonderful and waved as he left.

"Charming man," Aunt Sarah said, eying Graham carefully.

He was entirely focused on a piece of berry pie in front of him. When he did look up, his expression was carefree, devoid of any of the turmoil going on in my own mind. He turned to Aunt Sarah and Alice. "So, what are the things two newcomers to the city must do and see?"

Aunt Sarah suggested a theater, but Alice waved her away and carried on and on about the Statue of Liberty and the tallest skyscraper in New York City without seeming to take a single breath. Seeing her so excited about something after an evening of grumbles abated whatever annoyance I felt towards Graham for delaying my conversation with Edward Taylor. Because although I had come to the city to help Catherine, it also felt nice to be reunited with my family.

7

Graham knocked on the door of Aunt Sarah's house the moment we finished eating breakfast. I had just pushed away from the table, so full of fruit, eggs, and croissants that I wasn't sure I'd even be able to stand, when a servant led Graham into the room. He had traded in his uniform for a dark gray suit and vest, red tie, and black and white two-toned oxfords with a black fedora. He looked dashing, and Alice most certainly took notice.

"Mr. Collins, you look wonderful," she crowed, sitting up in the chair she had been slumped in, complaining about getting little sleep, only moments before. She turned to me. "What are you going to wear, Rose?"

I was in a pale blue walking suit and my brown low-heeled oxfords, and I had no intention of changing. "We are sightseeing, are we not? No need for a ball gown."

"You look beautiful as ever, Rose," Graham said, winking when Alice looked away.

Alice sighed. "I know just the outfit I would wear on a day like today."

"Subtlety was never a strength of yours." Catherine shook her head at her younger sister. "Don't let Alice fool you, Mr. Collins. She sees plenty of the city."

Graham smiled and made no move to invite her like I thought he might, and then the idea of spending the entire day alone with him settled over me. It felt oppressive like the heat of an Indian summer.

"Alice has not seen the city with me," I said, reaching a hand across the table to clutch Alice's fingers. "I would love for you to show me New York the way you see it. Would you come along with us?"

Catherine opened her mouth to argue, no doubt about to tell me that indulging Alice would only make it worse the next time she wanted to accompany me somewhere, but I would worry about that then. Right now, she would act as the perfect barrier between myself and Graham. Besides, she had been feeling left out of all the fun, and this seemed like the perfect way to include her.

Alice jumped up at once. "Give me ten minutes to change."

Then, she was gone.

Graham maintained the same relaxed smile while we waited for Alice, showing no sign of frustration with me for ruining what may have very well been his attempt at an outing for the two of us. And when Alice came down the stairs, head held high, Graham bowed low and extended an elbow for the two of us, leading us through the front doors like it had been his plan all along.

ALICE TOOK control of the day at once, telling the driver to head for one of her favorite shops. From there, we walked in and out of dress shops where Alice admired the luxurious fabrics and made several orders to be delivered to her aunt's house. Then, we stopped for tea at the only place in the city she claimed could rival the teashops in London.

"Where did you two meet?" Alice asked, hands clutching her delicate mug.

Graham was reclined in his chair, legs crossed, staring out the window toward the people passing on the street like he was a world away. But he answered quickly. "I was a dinner guest at Rose's hosts' home her first day in Simla. She joined me the next day to visit local ruins."

A shadow crossed over his face, and he blinked. The ruins where we became friends were also the ruins where I'd fought for my life. I didn't have to wonder whether Graham was remembering the last time we'd been there. Of course, he was. Especially since he had apologized to me several times since about arriving too late to be of any help to me. It was not Graham's responsibility to protect me, but I could not convince him of that, and I doubted I ever would be able to.

Alice frowned. "I always imagined you two meeting at a dance."

"Always?" I teased. "You only learned of his existence yesterday."

"Always since yesterday," Alice said, looking at me as though I had wounded her. I hid my smile in my coffee cup. Alice already had an older sister. She wasn't looking for yet another in me.

Graham looked over, his blond mustache tilting upwards in a thoughtful smile. "Rose and I had many adventures in India, but we never did manage to attend a social gathering where dancing occurred. Quite a shame, actually. I'm a wonderful dancer."

"And modest too."

He laughed. "Why should one be modest about their talents? I would not claim to be worthy of a competition, but I have many past dance partners who will vouch for my abilities."

"Write down their names, and I'll write to them one by one," I said. "Are you still so confident?"

He leaned forward, elbows resting on the table, eyes narrowed in a mischievous way. "I'll get you the list by this evening."

"I believe you, Mr. Collins," Alice said, reinserting herself into what had become a private conversation.

I leaned back in my chair, trying to understand the flutter in my stomach that started as soon as Graham narrowed his eyes at me. I took another long drink of tea, hoping the warmth would settle it, but nothing seemed to help. So, I ignored it.

AFTER TEA, we walked along the East River. Couples milled along in their afternoon dress, some already wearing their evening dinner attire, hurrying through the crowds towards whatever engagement awaited them. But we did not hurry. Alice paused to lean against the stone railing, peering down at the water dramatically, her new short hair getting caught by the wind off the river. I clung tightly to my own cloche hat, pulling it down further over my ears to keep away the chill. When Graham slipped out of his jacket and offered it to me, I wanted to refuse if only to keep from encouraging him in an affection I did not yet return, but a shiver worked its way down my spine and he settled it over my shoulders.

"I thought this would be our last stop for the day," he said. "Alice doesn't ever seem to weary, but I suspect you are tired."

I laughed. "Alice is young. I am not."

"You are hardly old," he said urgently, clearly afraid he had offended me. "But after a long sea voyage, I only assumed you would want time to rest."

I laid a hand on his shoulder and smiled. "Quite right you are. I have yet to see it, but I would be surprised if my Aunt's home did not have an impressive library tucked away somewhere. I would not hate curling into a comfortable chair with a book for the rest of the evening. Besides, we did not tell Aunt Sarah we wouldn't be home for dinner, so I'd hate to miss a meal she may have had prepared for us."

"And Catherine will probably be missing your company by now," he said. "She and her sister bicker more than anything else, but she seems to like you."

"It has not always been so." I remembered when I first arrived in London the cold reception I'd received from my cousin. My arrival meant her brother would not receive the inheritance my death would have given him, and though she later admitted it was unfair of her, she blamed me for their financial woes. In the end, everything sorted itself out, though not in the way anyone would have expected. "Our relationship grew over a long time, and I believe my time away the last few months has brought us even closer together."

Alice advanced towards a pigeon, her hand held out as though she had food in her palm, and when the pigeon came close, she reached out as though to grab it with both hands. I almost called out for her to stop, but the bird flew away before I had to intervene. As soon as the bird was gone, Alice turned quickly to look over her shoulder and see whether anyone had been watching her. I looked down at the ground, smiling. She was playing the role of a woman, but a child still lived in her breast.

Graham nodded slowly, stepping even closer to me as we ambled along, his elbow brushing my arm. "I do not know either of them well, but it seems Charles Cresswell has a calming effect on Catherine, as well."

"I know Charles just as well as you do," I admitted. "But Catherine has admitted as much to me. To my surprise, she is infatuated with the man. That isn't to say he is not worthy, only that I imagined my cousin with a much less genial man, if we are speaking frankly."

"May we always speak frankly to one another, Rose." Graham smiled down at me, nose wrinkled.

That fluttering feeling made itself known again, and I crossed my arms over my stomach to fight it back as Graham continued.

"When Catherine spoke of their meeting last night, it

seemed as though they had only known one another a few weeks," he said.

"That is my understanding, as well."

Graham paused, looking out over the water. Then, he tucked his hands behind his back. "They moved rather quickly. Do you know if there is a reason for that?"

I snapped my attention to him. "Are you asking me if Catherine had a physical reason for getting married so soon?"

It took Graham a moment to understand my meaning, during which time I realized that I had misunderstood his question. His face went red. "No, of course not. I would never do her the dishonor of suggesting that. I didn't mean—"

"My mistake. I misunderstood," I said kindly. "Catherine has not told me any specific reason other than that she loves him deeply, and I can tell from the way he looks at her that the feeling is mutual."

"They do seem to be very in love," he said. "Though, I do wonder whether it is possible to really know someone in such a short amount of time. He is older, so perhaps he is in more of a hurry than he would be if he and Catherine were the same age. Of course, I don't want to insult their relationship by speculating."

"Catherine would never forgive you for suggesting their forthcoming nuptials have to do with anything other than true love, but as you said, may we always speak frankly with one another," I laughed. "However, I do believe love is more than the amount of time you've known a person. It is possible to meet someone and know they are for you, and it seems that is what happened when Charles first saw Catherine."

I could feel Graham looking down at me, waiting for me to meet his gaze, but I did not. Instead, I watched Alice drop a rock into the river and then turn around and wave for the two of us to join her. I walked towards her immediately and Graham followed, a small smile playing on his lips the rest of the afternoon.

When he delivered us home, Alice hugged him, thanking him for one of her favorite days in the city so far. He assured her the pleasure was all his and then dipped his head to me. "Enjoy your book, should you find it, Rose."

He stepped across the threshold and onto the porch, but before the door could close, Aunt Sarah walked down the stairs.

"Leaving so soon, Mr. Collins?"

Graham stepped back inside and grabbed the hand she extended to him. "Not if you wish for me to stay."

"Such a charmer," she said, winking at me. "I would not want to keep you from any plans you may have this evening."

"I don't know anyone else in the city, so my social calendar is quite thin," he admitted.

Aunt Sarah clicked her tongue against the roof of her mouth. "Unacceptable. Such a dashing man should be on the scene, and if you are up for it, I will introduce you this evening."

Graham looked to me at the same time Aunt Sarah turned around. "I thought you would want to come, as well, Rose. I should have mentioned it sooner, but one thing you will come to learn about me is that I am scattered."

"To say the least," Alice whispered, earning a scathing look from her aunt. She quickly dashed up the stairs, stifling a giggle.

"Come where, exactly?" I asked.

Aunt Sarah laughed. "Right, of course. It is a party held by a dear friend of my late husband's. All the best of New York society will be there, and I'd love for you to make an appearance. With your youth and looks, you'll be the talk of the party. Another thing you will learn about me is that I love being the talk of the party. And since you are staying with me, I'll have the pleasure of introducing you to everyone. What do you say?"

I could practically hear the books calling to me from some hidden room in the back of the mansion. My feet ached from walking all day, and I felt weary down to my bones, but Aunt Sarah was grinning up at me hopefully, and even Graham looked excited at the prospect. And Aunt Sarah was letting me stay in her house indefinitely even though she was not my aunt at all. Attending one party with her seemed like the least I could do.

"It would be nice to meet more friends inside the city."

Aunt Sarah clapped her hands and wrapped her arm through mine. "We must get you ready at once. We'll leave in a few hours." Then, she turned to Graham. "And you will be her escort, won't you? You two make such a lovely pair."

Graham's eyes twinkled when he looked at me. "It would be my honor."

I'd been looking forward to a quiet evening alone—I'd had dreadfully few of those in the last year—but if attending one party would make both Sarah and Graham happy, how could I refuse? Besides, another opportunity to see Charles Cresswell interacting with his peers would be useful to my investigation.

Aunt Sarah practically pushed Graham through the door, telling him to go put on whatever he had that was best and return in an hour. Then, she dragged me up the stairs, telling me she had just the gown for me to wear. Once again, how could I refuse?

8

T he party was held only a few blocks from Aunt Sarah's house in a mansion quite similar to hers. Guests filled the space more easily than I would have imagined, and it forced one to remain close to one's group or be separated. Staying close did not seem to be a problem for Graham. His body was pressed against my arm from the moment he saw me standing in the entryway of Aunt Sarah's house.

The gown Aunt Sarah had for me was the nicest thing I'd ever worn, and both Catherine and Alice complained that she had never offered it to either of them.

"Because you do not have the right figures for it," she argued. "You are both beautiful, but Rose has the small chest a dress like this requires."

Aside from the embarrassment I felt about my family discussing my intimate body parts, I felt gorgeous in the gown. It was gold and shimmery with flowers beaded into the silk. The top cut low across my chest, revealing more of myself than I was usually comfortable with while still remaining appropriate, and the bottom ruffled out in a fuller skirt that ended below my knee. I wore a pair of white t-strap heels that wrapped around my ankle and carried a matching beaded handbag.

Graham's mouth slacked open when he saw me, and he didn't pick it up until we arrived at the party and the large number of guests distracted him. Even still, he couldn't stop complimenting me whenever I caught his attention.

"You are the most lovely woman in the room," he said over the sound of many conversations and live music that was coming from somewhere deeper in the house.

"You look wonderful, too," I said.

He wore a double-breasted tweed suit in a checkerboard pattern with a red tie and pocket square. In his Lieutenant uniform, he looked honorable and proper, but in civilian clothing, he had a new kind of mystery. I noticed women staring at him as we moved through the room, and it made it so I didn't mind him standing so close to me. Even though Aunt Sarah and I weren't related, it seemed I had a little bit of her in me. I didn't mind being the talk of the party.

Alice was not having as nice of a time. Since she did not have a suitor, she walked through the party on her aunt's arm, looking longingly at every couple she passed. At one point, I even saw her staring at her sister and Charles Cresswell without the usual disgust she seemed to reserve for them.

Charles, on the other hand, seemed to have overcome his strangeness from the night before. He kept one arm firmly around his beaming fiancé while he shook hands and spoke with everyone he passed. It was obvious he was a very well known and well-respected man in the city.

"I'm not accustomed to being around so many people," Graham said, scanning the room. "Simla seems quite small compared to this."

"Surely you are not so easily overwhelmed," I said, surprised by the flirtatiousness in my own voice.

He raised an eyebrow and extended his hand. "Surely not. Would you care to dance?"

Before I could accept, Alice rushed over and grabbed my hand. "Save me, Rose."

"From what?" I asked, looking around, expecting a villain to be lurking nearby.

"Aunt Sarah," she whined. "I can't meet a man with her on my arm. She treats me like a child. Let me stand with you and then everyone will be looking at me."

I was about to tell Alice that not everyone was looking at me and that she did not need to find herself a man, but before I could, Catherine joined our group. She leaned in so close her lips were almost pressed to my ear. "Charles is talking with several colleagues. Come join us and pay attention."

"Is something the matter?" I whispered back, averting my eyes from Alice's disapproving stare. She hated being left out of anything.

"Not yet," Catherine said breathily. "But you are here to help me, not dance."

I didn't see why I couldn't do both, but I turned to Graham with an apologetic smile. "My cousin thinks I should be introduced before any fun can be had. But I will claim that dance later."

"I will join you," Graham said, offering me his elbow.

"You do not have to," I said, almost hoping he wouldn't. Investigating Charles would be easier without Graham standing next to me as a distraction.

"I would be delighted to," he said. "Besides, your aunt seemed to think we should stick close together for a bigger impact on the party."

So, I followed Catherine through the crowd to where Charles was smiling and laughing with his friends, all of whom were at least fifteen years older than myself and Catherine, with Graham at my side and a pouting Alice trailing behind.

"Charles, dear," Catherine said, placing a hand on his shoulder. "May I interrupt to introduce my cousin?"

Charles stepped aside, allowing the four of us to enter the circle. "Of course. Gentleman, this is Rose Beckingham and Graham Collins. They only arrived in New York yesterday morning and are already meeting the likes of you all, so be kind to them."

The men all laughed in unison, and Graham joined in, seeming more comfortable than I'd ever seen him. In Simla, he had been cautious in social settings, careful not to draw too much attention to himself or stand out, but he seemed different in New York. He smiled easier, and I felt the city had already had a positive effect on his social skills. I wondered whether he wouldn't be disappointed when the time came for him to return to India and his duties.

"I have vowed to never leave New York again," one of

the men said to Graham. "I get terribly seasick and the food on those ships is hardly edible."

"Those are as good of reasons as any to settle down," Graham said. Then, he patted my hand. "Rose has travelled from Bombay to London, from London to Morocco, Morocco to Bombay, and Bombay to New York all within the last nine months."

The men in the circle looked at me, eyes wide.

"Whatever for?" a gray-haired man asked.

Speaking of the bomb that killed my family didn't seem like good party conversation, so I just smiled. "Travel keeps one from growing bored."

Catherine patted my back and nodded, clearly relieved I hadn't launched into the details of my life with this group of her future-husband's friends, and honestly, it was nice to not have to endure the sympathetic smiles they certainly would have offered if I'd told them the truth. Perhaps, New York would have a positive effect on me, as well.

Many of the men, mostly American, were interested in Graham's service as Lieutenant in the British army, and they quizzed all of us on the ways life in England differed from that in America.

"I've been in America long enough now I can hardly remember my life in London," Charles said.

"But you go back for frequent visits, right?" Catherine asked, an edge of worry in her voice.

Charles must have noticed her concern, as well, because he pulled her into his side and kissed her temple. "We will travel back as often as you like, Katie. Anything to make you happy."

The gray-haired man, whose name I'd learned was William Brown, stepped forward, head shaking. "With the way things are going, you may want to stay in America permanently."

Catherine's eyebrows drew together. "Why is that?"

"With Germany showing early signs that it may be once again on the rise." He shrugged, as if that explained it all.

"Surely, there won't be another war," she said. "They wouldn't be so foolish."

"Power can make anyone foolish," Charles said solemnly. Then, he gripped Catherine tighter. "But you should not worry. William has always been a pessimist about such things."

"And I'm usually right," William said.

"That is up for debate," another man in the group said, clapping his hand on William's shoulder.

"Germany has been admitted into the League of Nations less than ten years after the end of the war. If that does not worry you in the slightest, then you are all fools," William said.

"To being fools!" one man shouted, raising his glass in the air.

I didn't have a glass to raise, though I wasn't sure I would have toasted to something like that. Graham must have had the same thought and leaned down to whisper in my ear. "Would you like a drink?"

I smiled and nodded, and for the first time all evening, he left my side.

Without him pressed against me, I noticed Alice standing on the edge of the circle talking to a young man who looked to be in his early-twenties. Alice laughed at something he said and reached a hand up to twirl her hair before realizing she had cut it short and letting the hand fall to her side. I vowed to keep a close watch on her. I wanted to trust her judgment, but as much as she insisted she was a woman, she had enough child left in her for me to worry.

"I think forgiveness is a practice carried out far too little by men in power," Catherine said. "Ten years seems like a great deal of time to me. I did many things ten years ago I wouldn't dare do today."

Suddenly, a thin elderly man in a red velvet suit pushed his way into the circle. I immediately knew he had to be someone important because the men jostled to make room for him, and every eye seemed fixed on him.

"Time works differently between people and countries," the man said sharply. "Especially when the person in question is young."

Catherine's cheeks colored, and though I expected her to respond in defense of herself, she lowered her head and stood closer to Charles' side.

The man continued. "As an old man, it does not seem so long ago that I was at the Paris Peace Conference seeking out the appropriate punishment for Germany. And yet, even those weak financial punishments have been renegotiated twice since then."

"Though Germany needed to pay for their crimes," William said, "Europe and the world are better when they are not crippled under restitution."

"Their crimes," the man mused, eyes foggy and

focused on the ceiling. "I wonder if you would feel differently had their crimes affected you more personally."

William, who had seemed so staunch a debater only moments before, seemed to shrink from his words, and not long after, left the circle entirely. In fact, the group of men slowly began to slip away, finding different excuses for why they had to leave.

"Less than ten years of struggle is not justice," the old man continued, as though talking to himself. And based on the way the group of men had disintegrated around him, he almost was talking to himself. In a fit of irony, I wished Graham were nearby to offer me an easy method of escape.

At that moment, Aunt Sarah emerged from the crowd and walked straight for our group.

"Mr. Rooker," she said, greeting the old man. "I meant to introduce you to my new house guest, but it seems you have already met."

"Not officially," I said, stepping forward, noting that Charles and Catherine slipped away from the group the moment the attention had been shifted to me.

Aunt Sarah looked pleased and threw her arm around my shoulders. "This is Rose Beckingham. She is the niece of my sister, though I claim her as one of my own."

The man extended a hand to me, and I took it. He had papery skin, and his fingers were ice cold. "Albion Rooker," he said.

"Lovely to meet you," I smiled.

"This is Mr. Rooker's home," Aunt Sarah clarified.

My eyes widened in understanding. "Your home is

beautiful. Thank you so much for having me. Had I realized who you were I would have—"

"Run away like everyone else," he finished, mischief hiding in his milky white eyes.

I laughed more out of a sense of discomfort than any real desire to laugh. When Graham returned, he briefly shook hands with Mr. Rooker, smiling wider when he was introduced as my date for the evening. Then, before the conversation could take off again, Aunt Sarah turned to Graham and took his hands.

"Would you oblige an old woman and dance with me, Mr. Collins?"

Graham looked down at me for just a second—long enough for me to see the disappointment in his eyes—and then he obliged, leading her to the next room over where the furniture had been pushed aside to make room for dancing. This left me alone with Albion Rooker.

"I'm sorry," Mr. Rooker said, stepping closer now that we were the only two remaining of what had, only minutes before, been a good-sized group.

"Whatever for?" I asked.

"For giving you the impression that I am nothing more than a grumpy old man," he said, smiling and revealing a mouth of yellowed teeth. "Talking about the war, especially with younger men and women, upsets me. They are so short-sighted."

"I understand," I said, though I didn't really. I was one of the young women he was referring to.

"Justice, especially justice served on such a large scale, cannot be carried out in a matter of years. Or with a simple slap on the wrist. It takes time, patience," he said.

"We all have to be willing to sacrifice in order to create the world we want. Do you understand?"

"I think so," I lied.

"William spoke of Europe being stronger with a stable Germany, but a stable Germany is dangerous," he said, his voice growing stronger with every word. I could see the anger blooming in him. Even his eyes seemed to become clearer. "If we are unwilling to be uncomfortable for the sake of a better world, then what are we willing to be uncomfortable for? Then what can a better world really mean to us?"

I did not know what to say, and Mr. Rooker seemed to understand this. He sank down into his bones again, the fire fading from his eyes. "Forgive me, I have lost control of my tongue again."

"It is quite all right," I said, offering him a kind smile.

He returned it and sighed. "I lost both of my boys to the war. And losing my family that way, it makes it difficult to sit by while the people responsible go unpunished."

Now I truly didn't know what to say. But I knew what I felt.

Hadn't I experienced that exact feeling? That was why I'd gone back to Simla, why I'd put myself in harm's way —to bring justice where it seemed there wouldn't be any. I wanted to know who had killed the Beckinghams, and I wanted them to receive punishment. Mr. Rooker was seeking the same.

"And the idea that the war was long ago only reminds me that they are gone," he said sadly. "And every day, they are fading from people's minds."

"I understand," I said, reaching out to touch his elbow. The touch was light, but he seemed to wobble under it. "I know what it means to lose family in a terrible way. To want justice."

Mr. Rooker looked up at me as though seeing me for the first time, and then his face lit up with recognition. "Of course. Rose Beckingham. Sarah spoke to me about your past, and I remember reading of the bombing that killed your family. I was sad to hear of it."

"Thank you." My smile was tight, but genuine.

Our conversation shifted from the heavy topics of death and war to the architecture of the house and the year it was constructed. I did very little talking, instead letting Mr. Rooker tell me what he believed was important. He struck me as a lonely man. Why else would an elderly man throw such a lavish party? He was remarking on the artist who painted the murals on the ceiling, bent backwards for months to create the motifs around all the moldings, when Aunt Sarah and Graham returned. Her face was flushed from the exertion, but Graham looked just as unruffled as when he'd left.

"Now that your party has returned," Mr. Rooker said, turning and grabbing my hand, bending as low as his old bones would allow. "I am going to find a corner to sit down and watch the rest of the evening unfold. Lovely to meet you, Rose Beckingham."

"Is Mr. Rooker leaving so soon?" Graham asked.

"He probably needs to rest. His health has been failing for some time," Aunt Sarah said, releasing Graham's arm to me and almost twining us together.

"And I am too old to keep up with a skilled dancer like Mr. Collins, so I pass him off to you, Rose."

Graham smiled and nodded to my aunt. "You kept pace with me as well as any young woman could."

"I'm sure Rose would like to prove that statement false," she said, pushing us towards the dance floor. "Dance and be merry, you two. I'm going to rest."

There was no arguing with Aunt Sarah, and before I knew it, we were in the middle of the dance floor, kicking up our heels to the jazz band playing on a small stage in the corner. Aunt Sarah was right when she called Graham a skilled dancer, and it seemed his boasting before hadn't been so far off. As a servant in the Beckingham household for most of my youth, the only time I had to dance was when the real Rose Beckingham would ask me to help her practice her steps in preparation for an upcoming social event. I relied heavily on those practice sessions to keep up with Graham and look the part, but based on the smile on his face and the flush in his cheeks, I was doing a fine job.

Finally, the music slowed down and Graham pulled me close, both of us puffing to try and catch our breath.

"What did you and Mr. Rooker discuss?" he asked after several minutes of quiet swaying.

"It was a normal introductory conversation," I said. I didn't know why, but it felt rude to reveal the loss of Mr. Rooker's sons to Graham. I was sure their deaths were public knowledge, but it didn't feel like my information to share.

"Did you discuss your past?"

"Yes, but how did you know?" I asked, looking up at him. His blond mustache twitched down in a frown.

"There was a sadness in your face when we walked up. I guessed that was the reason."

His answer took me by surprise. Clearly, Graham knew me better than I understood if he could read my face so well. There was something comforting and unnerving about that thought.

"You guessed correctly," I said. "He heard of their deaths in the paper and recognized my name."

Graham studied me for a minute, and then pulled me closer, hiding his face from me. "I wish I could have known them all. I wish I could have seen you all together."

Had Graham actually met the Beckinghams, he would have known me as Nellie Dennet, if he had bothered to know me at all. I would have been on the periphery of his conversations with Rose. If she had taken a fancy to him, then I would have endured endless hours of her describing his long face, white blond hair, and broad shoulders. I certainly wouldn't have been dancing with him in a mansion in New York City.

"I wish so, too."

9

M uch to Catherine's annoyance, I spent very little time with her and Charles for the rest of the party. I had come to New York to help my cousin uncover the mystery of her fiancé's strange behavior, but the city was proving more intoxicating than I expected. Graham and I spent a large portion of the evening dancing, and when we stopped to rest, we sipped punch and allowed Aunt Sarah to introduce us to everyone who passed by where we stood. It was a long and lovely evening, filled with laughter and dancing, unlike any night I'd ever had.

As such, I did not wake up at my normal time the next morning. My body was weary from travel, exploring the city with Graham and Alice, and dancing all night. So, when I did finally open my eyes, I decided staying in bed longer was worth missing breakfast. And I had just dozed off again when three soft knocks sounded on my door.

Too lazy to get up, I called to the knocker. "Come in."

Aunt Sarah poked her head around the door. "I hope I haven't woken you. You are usually awake by now."

"I was already awake," I lied. "Can I help you with something?"

She crossed the room and perched on the end of my bed, her hands folded in her lap as though she was hiding something there. "I only wished to speak to you alone for a moment. I love your cousins dearly, but they are nosy girls. Especially Alice. I find her lurking just outside of doorways far too often to ever have a private conversation within my own walls again."

I laughed. "She does not like to be left out of anything."

"No, certainly not," Aunt Sarah agreed with a smile. Then, her face fell and she twisted towards me, one knee tucked up on my comforter. "I have something for you, Rose, and I hope it will not upset you."

I sat up, my curiosity piqued, and Aunt Sarah unfolded her hands and revealed a square of paper in her palm. After a moment of hesitation, she gave it to me. The square was worn around the edges from time, and I realized it was a newspaper clipping. The ink was starting to transfer and blur, but a few words stuck out to me. *Bombing. Extremist. One survivor. Beckingham.*

"I saved it," she said softly. "Not really knowing why until you arrived here. I just think you should know that their deaths were felt all over the world. Even across oceans. Your parents were beloved."

"Thank you," I said, tears welling in my eyes for reasons no one would understand.

"Oh dear, I have upset you," she said.

I reached out and took her hand. "You haven't. Truly. Thank you for welcoming me into your home and family. I appreciate this very much."

She squeezed my hand back and, sensing I needed time alone, made her exit.

When she left, I cried like I hadn't cried in ten years. Not for the Beckinghams or the bombings, but for my own parents. For the people who were murdered in their home and, aside from a few articles about the savagery of the crimes, whose deaths went unnoted. I would have liked to have something related to their deaths. To their lives. Something that showed anyone aside from me cared that they were dead and gone.

The motivation that had evaded me all morning surged through me at once, and I rolled out of bed and into a neutral-colored skirt, blouse and sweater—simple clothes that would go unnoticed on the street. Then, I slipped from my room and from the mansion without notice.

I didn't have to pay attention to where I was going as I walked. I knew where I was. Even though I hadn't been in the city for years, I could see the map of it in my head, and I followed the streets until they became more and more familiar. Until suddenly, I wasn't surrounded by mansions and luxurious shopping, but squat brick buildings with laundry hanging from the windows. Instead of fashionable clothes and fine fabrics, men and women walked past in simple cottons the color of the earth.

Five Points was radically different from Fifth Avenue, but as I walked, I saw it was also radically different from the Five Points of my youth. In the ten years I'd been gone, many of the tenements had been torn down, and government buildings had replaced them. The old roosts of criminals and gang members were now occupied by businessmen and government officials.

As a child in Five Points, I'd spent my youth looking over my shoulder, wondering when and where we would be robbed or assaulted. But now, children played games in the streets, giggling and rushing out of the way of oncoming cars, while their parents watched them from apartment windows. Five Points had become—if not safe —safer, at least.

I turned the corner, passing by a corner store where a man bought cigarettes while lighting a new one from his pocket, and walked down two more blocks before I stopped and looked across the street.

The building had been torn down, but I recognized the land. I recognized the slope of the city, the look of Manhattan behind it. My childhood home.

There was a bench bolted to the curb, and I sat down, staring up at the unfamiliar building that stood like a stranger where my home had once been. I'd imagined coming back to Five Points and sitting on the stairs I'd sat on with my brother. I'd imagined running into the same group of kids who used to play together, not out of friendship, but necessity because the streets could be so mean. Of course, that had been unrealistic. Things had changed. Me most of all. I was no longer Nellie Dennet, but Rose Beckingham, the daughter of a British official. An orphan—though I'd been an orphan regardless of my name.

I hadn't read the newspaper clipping after Aunt Sarah

gave it to me because it felt like a betrayal. Of myself, of my real parents. But now, sitting in the place where they had lived and died, I felt ready to let go. I pulled out the clipping and began to read.

The article relayed the events of the bombing that I knew more intimately than anyone, and then it devoted a section to the victims. The names of the servants who were in the car, Mrs. Beckingham's name and the organizations she did charitable work for, and then the largest section to Mr. Beckingham and his career.

I knew all of the information already, so I skimmed, disappointed that the reading of the article hadn't felt like a more monumental release of the emotions from my past. But then, my eye caught on something.

MR. BECKINGHAM PLAYED a significant role in the Paris Peace Conference in 1919, and many point to it as a defining moment in his career, when he made the move from a climber of the political ladder to a man who had scaled its heights.

I HAD ALREADY BEEN LIVING with and working for the Beckinghams at this point, but I was a young girl and the comings and goings of Mr. Beckingham were not a concern of mine. So, I did not recall his involvement in the Paris Peace Conference. And truly, even a week before, the information would have meant very little to me. But since meeting Charles Cresswell, the conference in Paris had begun to stand out as something of note. The conference and the decisions made there had even been a conversation at the party the night before.

What was I to make of this?

People had been moving past me on the sidewalk the entire time, but one shadow, lurking just behind my shoulder, caught my attention, and I startled and turned to see a man standing near the curb. He wore a black derby hat, his chin tipped low so I could not see his eyes, and carried a long cane. One I knew, from experience, had a blade hidden in the end.

Even before I saw the thin black mustache, one side tipped into a smile, I knew who the man was.

In a mix of astonishment and relief, I walked towards him. "Monsieur Prideaux."

He looked up at me, not at all surprised at my presence, and smiled. "My dearest Rose."

10

He looked less tan than he had in Morocco, but still had the swarthy air of a well-travelled man. His clothes were meticulous as ever, freshly-pressed, and he removed his hat, tucked it beneath his arm, and ran a hand through his dark hair.

"What are you doing here?" I asked, stopping on the sidewalk several paces away. I'd been moving towards him like a woman possessed, but the hypnosis broke when he said my name.

"Is that any way to greet an old friend?" he teased, his French accent thick. I'd become richly acquainted with it during our time together, but after a month away, it sounded stronger. "Especially a friend you abandoned in the middle of the night."

"Forgive me," I said, doing my best to smile, to keep the reunion lighthearted. "I actually left early in the morning."

He nodded, his smile becoming sharper. "Thank you for the correction. That does make all the difference."

We would discuss my sudden departure from Morocco, but not now. Not when Achilles Prideaux was standing on the street where I used to live in New York City. "You did not answer my question."

He sighed. "I am in New York on a case."

I blinked, waiting for him to continue, but it seemed as though he thought that answer sufficed. It did not. "What are you doing *here*?"

"Ahh." He tipped his head back as though suddenly understanding my meaning. He turned towards the building that stood where my family's home once had. "You know, the public library keeps a lot of newspapers. Even though I did not know the exact date of your parents' deaths, it did not take me long to find the article that discussed their murders. And within that article, I found your old address."

My heart thudded inside my chest like a bass drum. "Why would you want that?"

Achilles shrugged. "I'm not sure. Maybe it was the detective inside of me always searching for answers. Or maybe, I hoped I'd find you here."

"Did you know I was in the city, as well?" I asked, taking a small but noticeable step backwards. "Is that why you came here? To find me?"

"I hope you won't be offended when I tell you not to flatter yourself," he said, a smug smile on his lips. "My business in the city has nothing to do with you. However, I did hear from a trustworthy connection that you had left Bombay on a ship headed for America. It did not seem so unlikely that you would end up in the place where your story began."

I believed him. Though part of me was still uneasy at the sight of Achilles, a fixture of my new life, in a place so firmly rooted in my old life, I did not believe he was there for any nefarious purpose.

"That does not explain why you came here," I said. "What business could you have at Nellie Dennet's old apartment?"

Achilles looked at me for a long moment, and I could feel him stripping away Rose Beckingham, looking beneath the surface to where Nellie Dennet had been hidden away for so long. He was the only person who knew me as Nellie, who knew my secrets, and in that moment, I was keenly aware of the kind of power it gave him over me.

Finally, after a long moment, he shook his head and smiled. "Maybe you could answer a few of my questions now."

I nodded and walked back to the bench I'd been sitting at. I felt suddenly unsteady on my feet. Achilles sat beside me, stretching out his legs in front of him, his hands folded one on top of the other on the crook of his cane.

"Why did you leave?"

The haughtiness was gone from his voice. The question, short and simple, revealed a great deal of vulnerability, and I looked away from him, staring down the street. "I was in Morocco to assist you, Achilles. I wanted to be free from the role I was playing, not take on another, behaving like some dutiful wife."

"I never treated you that way," he said sharply, seeming almost embarrassed by the suggestion.

"No," I agreed. "Though, with time, I believe you would have."

He said nothing, and I felt bad at the idea that I had offended or hurt him. Our complicated past aside, I had no desire to wound him.

"I left because I wanted to salvage what remained of our friendship," I said.

He looked at me for a moment, eyes wide, and then shook his head. "Forgive my disbelief, Miss Beckingham, but when you fled from my company in the cover of darkness, I considered if the end to our friendship."

"Surely your feelings are not so precious as to be wounded by only that," I teased. Our relationship had always been biting, and I did not want to set the precedent for anything less now. Though emotions had threatened to turn our friendship into something more meaningful, and I was certain Achilles was remembering those feelings now, there had not been time nor space for those feelings to mature. So, I still considered us to be friends. I hoped he felt the same.

"The nature of my feelings would surprise you," he said more seriously than I expected.

I did not want to know what that meant, so I carried on as though he hadn't spoken at all. "Now, it is once again your turn to answer a question. What are you doing here?"

"I told you," he said. "I thought you might be here."

"Yes, but why would you want to see me?" I asked.

He raised a dark eyebrow at me. "You have said we are friends. Don't friends visit one another?"

I sighed and moved to smooth my hands down the

front of my skirt when I remembered the newspaper article in my hand. When I looked back up at Achilles, an idea was forming in my mind.

Achilles' eyes narrowed. "You have had an idea."

"Excuse me?" I asked.

"I recognize that look in your eyes. It almost always accompanies you doing something reckless."

I felt my face flush at the reality that Achilles knew me so well, but I ignored it and shook my head. "Nothing reckless. I only realized that your following me may be quite beneficial to a case I am working on."

"I am not following you," Achilles said, his stern tone accompanied with a finger point. Then he relaxed back into the bench. "And I should have known you were on a case. Though, I must say, good manners should prohibit you from asking me for a favor so soon after our reunion, especially after the way we left things."

"No one has ever accused me of good manners."

Achilles almost smiled. "What is troubling you, Rose?"

"Nothing too serious, I assure you," I said. "I am assisting a friend in a case, and I am in need of—"

"What case?" he asked.

"It is a private matter." Catherine had asked for privacy, and though I knew I could trust Achilles, I did not want to betray my cousin's trust.

"I know of your activities in Simla," he said softly.

I'd wondered whether Achilles had heard news of what I'd done there. Who I had killed.

"I am a grown woman, Achilles. I do not need your watchful eye."

"I know." He shifted on the bench, crossing one leg over the other.

"And yet, you have, what? Had me followed? Was I under constant watch during my time in Simla?" For a moment, the idea that Graham could have been working for Achilles, sending him updates, crossed my mind, but I dismissed it immediately. Graham's motives and motivations were much too transparent. I would have suspected him of suspicious connections early on in our friendship.

"I have connections everywhere," Achilles said. "Some of them who knew of our friendship reached out to me. I only learned of the death of Mr. Barlow after the fact. You are lucky to be alive."

Achilles had already admitted to knowing of my whereabouts, but the reality that he knew where I was and what I had been doing unnerved me. I'd wondered about him during my time in Simla, but he had not needed to worry about me. I wondered if he knew of Graham Collins. "Disposing of two international assassins hardly seems like luck, wouldn't you agree?"

"You are very skilled, but I wish you would not think yourself invincible. Taking on another assassin alone would be unwise."

"Then you'll be pleased to know I'm no longer on the hunt for assassins," I said coolly. "But I am on the hunt for information."

"As I'm sure you know, I am at your disposal, Miss Beckingham."

For a short while in Morocco, Achilles called me Nellie. The name had felt strange after so long without it, but now, it felt strange to hear him call me Miss Beckingham. With Achilles, I was never quite sure who I was supposed to be.

"As we've already discussed, you have many useful connections," I said, sounding only slightly bitter. "I wonder if you could reassign the connections who have been watching me to another task."

"No one was assigned to watch you," he spat, growing frustrated with the repeated charge of having me followed.

I continued as though I hadn't heard him, though my tone softened. "I need a list of every person in attendance at the 1919 conference in Paris."

"That is an impressive task." He sat tall as if ready to rush from the bench and get to work. Achilles truly was a detective at heart. He was driven by mystery, drawn to finding answers no matter how difficult it might be.

"It is," I said. "The question is whether it is impossible?"

Achilles had warned me against thinking myself invincible, but he had a bad habit of considering himself capable of anything. So, even the suggestion that this task was too complex would strengthen his resolve to see it through. I knew this and utilized it to my advantage.

"Of course, it is not impossible," he said. "But it may take longer than you like."

"As soon as possible is all I ask."

"That is *all you ask*," he said, slightly mocking. "You have asked a great deal of me since we became friends eight months ago."

"Only eight months?" I mused, biting my lip to stop

from smiling at his admission that we were still friends. "It seems we have been friends for longer than that."

He hummed an uncommitted response. "And I would like to be friends for longer, so promise me you will be cautious."

"I always am, Achilles," I lied. We both knew that was not true.

Achilles stood up, tapped his cane on the ground, and replaced his hat on top of his head. When he looked down at me, his eyes were cast in shadow, but his lips were curled upwards beneath the thin line of his mustache. "Should I reach out to you at the home where you cousins are staying or would you like for our communication to be more discreet?"

I should have known he knew where in the city I was staying. He had pretended as though finding me at my parents' old apartment was a lucky coincidence, but I wondered whether he hadn't followed me.

"I do not want anyone to know we are once again in communication," I said, thinking of Alice and Catherine who had hinted they believed me and Achilles to be in love, but also Graham. I did not want him to know of Achilles. In many ways, they were two sides of the same coin, one dark and one light. One an international man of mystery, the other an open book. I had no desire for them to meet. "But I trust you can be discreet however you choose to reach out again."

"I will speak to you soon, Rose." He nodded once and then walked down the street. I watched him go, and when he turned the corner, I almost couldn't believe he'd really been there at all.

11

I expected Graham to be waiting for me at Aunt Sarah's when I returned, but instead I found Catherine, Alice, and Aunt Sarah in the sitting room, a tower of biscuits, scones, and pastries in front of them. As soon as my presence became known, they waved me into the room.

"You are finally home," Alice said, as though we had arranged a meeting.

"I thought we'd have to send one of the servants out to search for you," Catherine said, looking half-serious.

Only Aunt Sarah stayed quiet, smiling and patting the seat next to her on the velvet sofa, which I gladly took. "What is this? Are you having a tea party?"

"We are not children," Alice snapped, annoyed at my dismissal of what she clearly saw as a sophisticated affair. "We are helping Catherine plan her wedding."

Catherine looked away at this, focusing intently on the cold fireplace.

"I don't know anything about weddings," I admitted. "I'm not sure how much help I'll be."

"You are a woman of taste, aren't you?" Alice asked.

"Depending who you ask," I teased.

Aunt Sarah laid a hand on my shoulder. "Of course, you are, dear. All three of you have exquisite taste. You'll plan a wonderful event."

"You are helping, too, Aunt Sarah," Alice said. "There is a lot to think about, and you have more experience than any of us."

"Because I'm an old woman?" Aunt Sarah asked, one eyebrow lifted.

Alice's eyes went wide and panicked for a moment before Aunt Sarah laughed. "I'm the only one here who has actually been married. I know that is what you meant."

Catherine had promised an explanation of Aunt Sarah's situation, but there hadn't been time. Not with Charles' strange behavior and Graham showing up at every spare moment. But it was simple enough to deduce that her husband had died, and his inheritance went to Aunt Sarah. She never spoke of having children, and I hadn't noticed any sign of pictures or portraits of them throughout the house, so it was just her now. Her family history made it clear why women's rights was an important issue for her.

"Exactly," Alice said, clearly relieved. Then, she pulled out a piece of paper where she had scribbled a list. "First, would you like to be married in London or Somerset?"

There was a long pause and everyone turned to look

at Catherine, who was clutching her China cup with both hands, eyes vacant and staring.

"Catherine?" Alice prodded, poking her sister with a finger.

Catherine jolted and clutched at her arm. "Ouch. Why did you do that?"

"This meeting is to assist you with wedding plans," Alice snapped. "The least you could do is pay attention. Where would you like to be married?"

"I haven't thought much about it," Catherine said with a sigh.

Alice shook her head, her short brown curls bouncing around her ears, disappointed. "As I see it, there are only two options: London or Somerset."

Catherine glanced at me quickly before looking back at the floor, and I could see something was wrong. Clearly, this gathering had not been her idea. She had no desire to discuss wedding plans, which meant something must have happened with Charles to have her more upset than usual.

"That is a rather large decision," I said, jumping in. "Somerset is lovely, but London has many benefits, as well. Perhaps, we could start with a simpler decision."

Alice looked at her sister for a moment, waiting to see if Catherine would contradict my decision. When she didn't, instead taking a long sip of her tea, Alice looked back to her list, her finger skimming down to the bottom of the paper. "Most of the decisions depend upon the location. Decorations, seating, wedding date—all decisions that are dependent on whether the wedding will be in a church or at the country estate."

"Charles and I will set our own wedding date," Catherine said.

"What about a dress?" Alice asked with a slump of her shoulders. "We could have one made here in New York and take it with us back to London. Or you could have it done in London, though depending on the date you set, the designer might not be able to get it done in time. Charlotte Faybury has been doing our dresses for years, but I have never seen her take on an elegant gown."

"Maybe," Catherine said, barely paying attention.

Alice sat on the edge of the sofa, practically bouncing with excitement. "I saw a wonderful dress shop while I was exploring the city with Graham and Rose. I could take you there and see if any of the designs jump out at you. If not, I'm sure they could make something to your specifications. Women in London are always saying the best fashion comes from New York, anyway. Your gown would be the envy of everyone."

"There are many good designers here," Aunt Sarah agreed. "I'd be happy to introduce you to my favorites."

Alice gasped. "Or Paris. We could have father send us to Paris. Can you imagine?"

"No, I can't," Catherine said, but Alice was so wrapped up in her ideas, scribbling down more items on her list, that she didn't know the glassy look in her sister's eyes.

"Where are you two going to live?" Alice asked, brows knit together in concern. "You will live in America, won't you? Will you live in Charles' house? It is barely big enough for the two of you, so I don't see how there will be room for guests. How am I supposed to come stay with you if you don't have a proper guest room?"

"My house is plenty big," Aunt Sarah said. "You can stay with me when you come to the city."

Alice smiled at her aunt, but did not look convinced. "Catherine, you should tell Charles to find a new house."

"Charles may not want a new house," Catherine said.

"He would do anything to make you happy, and a bigger house would make longer visits much more comfortable for everyone."

Catherine's fingers were nearly white around the cup, and I worried she would shatter it in her hands.

"I just remembered," I said, moving to stand up. "I made plans with Graham today. Maybe we could reschedule wedding planning for another afternoon?"

Alice shook her head. "Graham already came by, and I sent him away."

"He came by?" I asked.

"You sound surprised," Alice said. "I thought you had plans?"

"We did. He must have come early."

Alice pursed her lips. "Regardless, I told him the women of this family needed to spend time together without any manly company and he said he would call on you tomorrow."

Perhaps, Alice was feeling more left out than I'd realized to go as far as to plan this event and turn Graham away. She seemed so smitten with him over the last few days that I would have thought her incapable of sending him away.

"Now," Alice said, clapping her hands together in excitement. "Do we have thoughts on flowers? I like white lilies, but I know Catherine prefers roses. Does Charles have a favorite flower? Men don't usually care about these kinds of things, but it doesn't hurt to ask."

"I don't know," Catherine said.

Alice's brow furrowed in frustration, and I could practically see her expectations clashing with the reality of this lackluster planning meeting. Catherine was barely participating, and Alice had gone to great lengths to make it a nice event. "Catherine, I don't mean to be rude, but do you even want to get married?"

Catherine's head snapped up, her blue eyes icy. "For not meaning to be rude, your words certainly are effective."

"I'm sorry," Alice said, not sounding sorry in the least. "But I have never met a bride less interested in her own nuptials. I thought you would enjoy talking through the details."

"I'm just..." Catherine paused and swallowed. "I'm just not sure."

"What about dinner?" Alice asked, looking over her list. "Do we want to hire it out or would the kitchen staff suffice?"

Suddenly, Catherine jolted to her feet, a bit of tea splashing out of her cup and onto the floor. Alice pulled her foot away from the spill and studied her slipper to make sure it was clean.

"I'm tired," Catherine said, setting her cup on the table. She looked at us for a moment, blinking back the beginnings of tears, and then rushed from the room before anyone could respond.

"I do not understand her," Alice said, throwing her list on top of an iced scone.

"She said she was tired," I said, trying to ease away the tension. "I'm sure there is nothing else to it."

"No," Aunt Sarah said, shaking her head. "Something is wrong. Catherine has grown quiet these last few weeks."

"Has something happened between her and Charles?" Alice asked. "I would guess they had called off the wedding except they were never apart last night. Have I done something wrong?"

"Catherine has never been the type to stay quiet when it came to trouble between the two of you," Aunt Sarah said. "I'm sure it isn't you."

Alice crossed her arms over her chest, looking more like a small child than I had ever seen, and pouted out her lower lip. "I don't care anything about wedding planning, but I made an effort for her sake. It would be nice if she could make an effort in return."

"I don't think it has anything to do with you, Alice," I said.

Alice looked unconvinced and stared stonily at her list that was absorbing more oil from the sugary icing with every second.

"I'll go talk with her," I said, standing up. "I will try to see if I can tell what is going on."

Alice huffed. "She would rather speak to you, anyway, I'm sure."

I wanted to comfort Alice, but I couldn't without revealing Catherine's secret and my purpose in New York City, so I just slipped from the room and walked up the stairs to Catherine's door. She opened it before I could knock.

"I sense there might be something wrong," I said, closing the door behind me.

Catherine opened her mouth before thinking better of it. She moved to the door and yanked it open, looking around the corner to see if Alice was lurking outside. When she closed it, she grabbed my hand and pulled me to the far corner of the room nearest the window.

In the daylight, I could see the dark circles under eyes, the hollows along her cheekbones. She looked more worn and gaunt than I had ever seen her. "Things are growing worse."

"With Charles?" I asked.

She nodded.

"You two seemed fine at the party last night. Did something happen afterwards to upset you?"

"No," she said. "Well, yes. Everything is upsetting. The man you saw at the party was an imposter."

I narrowed my eyes. "What do you mean? I saw him, Catherine. It was Charles. Do you mean he isn't really Charles Cresswell?"

She rolled her eyes. "I mean that the jovial man shaking hands and delighting the guests is only for show. As soon as we are alone, Charles is solemn and silent. He spends his time staring into dark corners and ignoring my questions. It feels like he is a world away, and I'm not sure what has changed. He won't tell me anything."

"You've asked him directly?" I asked.

"Of course," Catherine snapped, a bit of her old fire returning. "He tells me it is nothing, but I can feel that things are different. He looks at me the way he always has, but it feels like some secret force is draining the life from him, and slowly, he is slipping away."

"Perhaps," I said, approaching the next words cautiously. "You do not know Charles as well as you think you do."

Catherine looked up at me, her eyes focused. Her words came out biting. "What do you mean?"

I took a deep breath. "Only that you've only known him a short while. Is there any chance he has always been distant and cold, but the first few weeks with you were different? Perhaps, this descent is less of a change and more of a fall back into old habits?"

I didn't know that I truly believed this, but it seemed like a possibility worth looking into as much as anything else. Catherine, however, disagreed.

Without saying a word, she turned away from me, walked across the room, and opened her bedroom door. "If that is the most help you can offer me, I must ask you to leave my room immediately."

I realized my mistake at once. I crossed the room and pushed the door shut. "It was merely a suggestion."

"It was an insult," she snapped.

"You're right, I'm sorry. You know your fiancé better than I do, and I shouldn't have suggested otherwise."

Catherine crossed her arms, looking very much like Alice had only a few minutes ago downstairs, and looked down at the floor. "Does this mean you don't know how to help me, then?"

"Absolutely not," I said quickly. "In fact, I reached out to a contact for help just this morning."

Catherine stiffened. "You told someone?"

"Nothing specific," I amended. "They are helping me gather information. I haven't revealed your plight to anyone."

She took a breath, relieved, and then looked up at me. Her eyes were shiny with unshed tears and her lower lip trembled. "Do you think you can help?"

I reached out and grabbed her hands, folding them inside my own. "I will do my absolute best. I can assure you of that much."

She stared at me for a moment as if to see if I was being honest, and then she nodded once. "Thank you, Rose. Now, could you leave me? I'd like to be alone for a bit."

As soon as I stepped into the hallway, I heard a male voice. I was prepared to reach the top of the stairs and see Graham—defiant of Alice's banishment—standing in the entryway. However, I was met with a man I did not know.

He was a young man who could not be older than his early twenties, and his red hair was combed starkly to one side, emphasizing the square shape of his face. Everything else about him was square, as well. Even his fingers—adjusting the tie around his neck—looked to be squared off on the tips. He shifted nervously from one foot to the other as Aunt Sarah spoke with him.

"You say you met Alice last night at the party?" She asked. "I must not have had the pleasure of meeting you, then."

"Aunt Sarah," Alice groaned, tugging on her aunt's arm. "He has only come for tea."

"And who is stopping him?" Aunt Sarah asked innocently, raising an eyebrow at the man as she stepped aside and motioned him and her bubbly niece into the sitting room. "There are treats of every kind and more in the kitchen, so eat your fill. I certainly shall."

The man stepped into the sitting room and Alice pulled her aunt aside. "You aren't coming with us, are you?"

"It is my home, dear," Aunt Sarah reminded her sharply.

Alice looked like she wanted to argue, but thought better of it. Just then, she saw me standing at the top of the stairs. Her eyes widened.

"Not you, too," she begged. "Please."

Caught out, I moved quickly down the rest of the stairs. "I thought today was for us girls to get together. Men aren't allowed, remember?"

Aunt Sarah beamed. "I do remember someone saying those very words when it came to the company of a certain Lieutenant."

"That was—" Alice searched for the words and then groaned. "Different. He is here to see me, and I'm being rude."

She disappeared into the sitting room, and Aunt Sarah grabbed my hand. "Are you sure you can't stay? I plan to tease her ruthlessly."

"As much as I want to see that, I'm afraid I have other business to attend to."

She waved me on and then walked into the sitting

room with an airy grace. "I have many childhood stories about our lovely Alice here. Did she have the opportunity to tell you about the time she lifted her dress above her head and showed my poor deceased husband her under-garments? God rest his soul."

"I was only a baby," Alice corrected.

I shut the front door softly, quite ashamed of how much I enjoyed Alice's torment.

I DIDN'T REALLY HAVE any business to attend to, but staying inside the house felt stifling. As much as Graham's constant presence had been an obstacle, it had also been a distraction. But now, left alone, waiting for Achilles to reach out with information that might or might not be helpful, I felt as though I was floundering.

Wandering the familiar streets of the city where I was born brought a sense of comfort that little else had in the previous year. Mingled with the comfort, however, was a sense of loss. I had been cast out of my home and life by a terrible act of violence as an orphan with no one in the world to claim me. In the years since then, I had survived, but nowhere ever felt as much like home as New York. Except, now that I was back, I couldn't help but notice the changes; the many ways the city had carried on without me.

It was this desire for a sense of familiarity that led me from the mansions of Fifth Avenue to the industrial heart of the city to the low-class neighborhoods that huddled in the haze just beyond them. And there, I found a building that had not changed at all in the many years I'd been gone.

The Sisters of Sorrow Orphanage for Lost Girls cut a sharp silhouette against the sky. The spire of the chapel sliced across the sky like a sword, stretching so high I had to strain my neck to take it all in. The stone façade was dirty and dingy from the smoke of the warehouses nearby and it didn't look like anyone was making any effort to keep it clean. When I lived in the orphanage, cleaning the stones by hand had been a punishment for naughty children. Either the sisters had moved on to worse punishments or the girls living within the walls now were better behaved than me and my friends had been.

I walked down the sidewalk, peering through the first floor windows to try and catch a glimpse of anyone inside, but saw no one. I even began to wonder whether the orphanage wasn't permanently closed, but when I pushed on the wrought iron gate between the public sidewalk and the traffic-worn stairs that led to the double wooden doors, the gate swung open without resistance. So, I stepped inside.

My memories of playing on the front steps and in the small patch of grass in front of the chapel were vivid, and being back there seemed to bring the memories even more prominently into my mind. However, I could not see the faces of the other children. Despite spending all of my time with the other orphans, I could not remember any of their names, and I could not recall any of their faces. It was almost as if they had been wiped from my memory entirely.

"May I help you, Miss?"

I startled and turned to see a young woman in a nun's habit standing on the top step, one of the wooden doors behind her standing open. Her hands were folded modestly in front of her, and her face was tilted down. As much as she tried to hide herself, her eyes were an arresting blue. At once, a flash of memory came to me. I saw the nuns leading lines of little girls to meal times and chapel. I saw them standing in the doorway of the large room where we all slept, fingers held to their mouths to tell us to quit whispering and go to sleep.

And in my memories, I saw this nun's face, though I knew it to be impossible. She was far too young to have worked at the orphanage while I'd been staying there.

"Miss?" she repeated when I failed to respond. She looked me up and down, taking in my fine attire. "Are you here about a particular child?"

"Oh, no," I said, trying to think of the right words to say.

"Just a visit, then?" she suggested kindly, almost as if she was trying to help me. "Our girls are very well behaved. Any would make a fine addition to a family or home staff."

I nodded and smiled. If I told the woman I had returned to the orphanage because I had once stayed there, she would want to know my name, and surely she would have questions about my accent. And if I told her I had no business there at all, she would be suspicious of my lurking.

"Would you care for a tour?" the woman asked. "I am Sister Elizabeth."

"Yes, please," I said, deciding at once that a tour would be the least suspicious thing I could do.

I followed Sister Elizabeth through the front doors and into the narrow entryway. The chapel doors stood straight ahead, thrown open for anyone passing by to stop and light a candle should they feel the urge. The Sister paused as if to allow me a moment in the chapel should I want it, but when I made no move to walk inside, she continued down the hallway towards where I knew the cafeteria would be.

She recited facts about the building and its history as we walked, discussing how many girls lived within its walls and their daily activities and curriculum, but I could hardly pay attention. Instead, I stared down at my fine Oxford heels on the scuffed floor, remembering the threadbare slippers I'd worn as a girl—the only pair I'd had to my name after my parents' murder. I studied each window as we passed, remembering the hours I'd spent gazing from these very windows, wondering when I would be able to move beyond them and see the world.

Sister Elizabeth showed me the cafeteria where a small collection of girls were helping clear away the last remnants of lunch. Each of the girls looked up as I entered, their eyes on me like wolves startled in the woods, wondering if I was friend or foe. I smiled at them, hating that I might be giving any of them a false sense of hope.

I remembered the feelings that would rise in me when anyone came through the front doors, wondering if I would stand out. If they would see me, want me, love me.

In the end, I'd been given a position instead of a family. And though Rose Beckingham had become like family to me over time, the Beckinghams were never my parents. I never had the kind of love and comfort I'd dreamt of and longed for each night in my bed.

I blinked away the mistiness in my eyes, overwhelmed by emotions I had not dwelt on in a very long time.

As we left the cafeteria, Sister Elizabeth looked over at me and then down at the floor. Then, she looked up again, eyes narrowed. When I met her gaze, she flushed.

"Forgive me, Miss. It is only that you look quite familiar. Is this your first time here?" she asked.

"Yes," I said with a smile, hoping to put the conversation to rest.

"Forgive me," she repeated. "I've been here a long time. Since I was a girl, actually."

My eyes went wide, and I was grateful Sister Elizabeth had not been looking at me to see my expression. Since she was a girl? "You lived in this orphanage?"

She nodded. "Since birth. The Sisters were the only family I ever had."

Her blue eyes were bright and clear as the sky on a spring day, and I could almost imagine the blonde hair beneath her habit. It would be darker now, no doubt. Not the vibrant white blonde curls she'd had as a child. But still, I knew it would be blonde. I had recognized Sister Elizabeth not because she looked like any of the nuns who had served the orphanage during my time there but because we had lived there together.

Her bed had been four down from mine in the dormi-

tory. She shared her desserts with new girls who came to
the orphanage, trying to comfort them during their first
day in a new place. She had given me half of her sweet-
bread the day I first arrived. I'd been too upset to eat it or
anything else on my plate, but she had extended it to me
nonetheless.

That memory had been lost to me before walking
through the doors and seeing her, but now I wondered
how I could have forgotten her at all.

Sister Elizabeth stared at me, her eyes narrowed and
suspicious, and I shifted from one foot to the other
nervously. I needed to leave. Coming back to the
orphanage had been silly. A risk with no reward. She
opened her mouth to say something, but was cut off by a
voice further down the hallway.

"Sister Elizabeth, do we have company?"

I turned to see another nun walking towards us. Her
hands were folded behind her back, but her shoulders
were broad, back straight. She walked with a kind of
pride I'd only seen in one nun.

"Sister Martha," Sister Elizabeth said in way of both
greeting and introduction. Though, the woman needed
no introduction. I remembered her well enough. She had
been the woman who connected me with the Beckingham family. She had secured my position with them
as a companion for their young daughter. "This is..."
Sister Elizabeth paused and then chuckled to herself. "I
just realized I never asked for your name, Miss."

It was funny seeing Sister Martha now compared to
the memory I had of her. As a child, she had been an
ancient woman. She was so far removed from being a

child that I wondered whether she could have ever been a child at all. Now, however, I realized she was no older than Aunt Sarah. When I lived in the orphanage, she must have only been in her forties or fifties. Certainly, not elderly. Then or now.

Which meant her memory would be sharp. Just as I remembered her and Sister Elizabeth, there was a chance she would remember me. A chance she would remember Nellie Dennet, the poor girl she had sent away to India only to have her blown to bits in a bombing. Had she heard of the accident? Would she have kept up with my placement so closely or bothered to remember my name? I had no way of knowing, and I was not going to see my entire life destroyed once again because of my own foolish mistake.

"I've just remembered," I said, taking a step away, moving backwards down the hallway. "I have to be going. I have a meeting across town."

Sister Elizabeth furrowed her brow and frowned. "You are leaving?"

"I'm sorry," I said, turning my head to the side to keep them from getting a better view of my face than they already had. "I will return soon."

"You are sure you must go?" Sister Martha asked, moving a bit faster towards me. Although I knew it unlikely, I thought she would rush forward and stop me from going.

"I am," I said, walking away, glancing back over my shoulder once to wave. "Thank you for the tour, Sisters. Goodbye."

I fled the building like I had wanted to many times in

my youth, rushing down the stairs and back onto the public sidewalk. I looked over my shoulder several times before I was confident no one was following me.

Seeking familiarity, I'd returned to the locations of my youth and nearly exposed myself and my deception. In one instant, the life I'd spun for myself over the last eight months could have vanished. As I walked back towards luxurious mansions where Aunt Sarah lived, I swore that I would not be so foolish again. New York City had not been my home. It had been the home of Nellie Dennet, and she was dead.

12

A lice's red-haired suitor visited again early the next morning and thoroughly distracted her from wedding planning, meaning, aside from her excited chatter and giggles, the house was quiet. Charles was busy with work, so Catherine stayed in her room except for meals, and Aunt Sarah sat at her desk and penned letter after letter to a local board she hoped to persuade to support the National Woman's Party.

Since Achilles and I had made no formal arrangement in terms of when or how he would reach out to me with the information about the Paris Peace Conference, sitting and waiting for him to make contact seemed fruitless, so I grabbed a book from Aunt Sarah's extensive shelves and read for most of the day. My excursion to the orphanage the day before had made me cautious about venturing too far beyond the constraints of Fifth Avenue anytime soon. I did not want to go anywhere Nellie Dennet would be recognized.

Late that afternoon when the servants were beginning preparation for dinner, someone knocked on the
front door. Alice, expecting her beau, rushed to the door
before even the servants could get to it, and threw the
door wide. She visibly deflated when she saw it was
Graham Collins.

"It's for you, Rose," she said, huffing away from the
door and dropping down on the sofa next to me. I put my
book away and went to properly greet Graham.

"Sorry for my cousin's manners," I said, not
mentioning that Graham had shown up once again
without any prior notice, which was not the best display
of fine manners.

"I thought Alice liked me," he said from the side of his
mouth, the words muffled. "Have I done something to
upset her?"

"You are not a young American with red hair," I said.

Graham's brow furrowed in confusion, but he did not
ask for any further explanation.

"To what do I owe the visit?" I asked, stepping aside to
welcome him into the entrance hall.

He moved past me and then spun around quickly,
extending a bouquet of flowers that had been hidden
behind his back. "For you, Miss Beckingham."

"They are lovely," I said, smelling the bouquet as I
accepted it. "But unnecessary."

"I heartily disagree. Flowers are always necessary
when asking a woman out on a date." Graham's face split
wide in a smile. Suddenly, I noticed the nervous fidgeting
of his feet and hands, the shakiness of his lips as he
smiled. Graham was nervous. Quite nervous, in fact.

Alice appeared unexpectedly in the doorway. Apparently, her interest in Graham had once again been piqued. "You're asking Rose on a date?"

"Alice," I scolded, shooing her away with a wave.

Then, as if Alice's audience was not enough, Aunt Sarah walked into the room. "Graham, are you staying for dinner? We have not had the pleasure of your company for the last couple of days."

"No, he can't stay," Alice said. "He is taking Rose out to dinner."

Aunt Sarah turned and saw the flowers and Graham, smiling and nervous, and cupped a hand over her heart like she was afraid it would leak out of her chest. "Oh my, it is about time, isn't it? I knew you two were more than friends."

"Aunt Sarah," I said even more severely than I had scolded Alice.

"Now you understand how I feel," Alice said in a low whisper that was still audible to everyone in the room.

"I actually have not asked anyone to dinner," Graham said, smiling, though I could tell by the pinch of his mouth that he was disappointed with the way things were going. He smiled at me and winked. "Not yet, anyway."

Suddenly, I didn't want Aunt Sarah or Alice to leave. I wished they would stay and insist he stay for dinner. That way we could eat all together in the dining room, and I would not have to contemplate my feelings for Graham.

I was grateful to him for caring so much about my safety, even if his concern did make him a nuisance a large portion of the time. And with the endless changes in my life, it was nice to have a constant friend. But could I see him as more than that? Would my lifestyle be conducive to a relationship? I tried to imagine dinner dates and dancing amidst my sneaking around and covert meetings, and the image refused to form.

"Alice," Aunt Sarah said, hurrying across the entryway and wrapping an arm around her youngest niece. "Come sit with me until dinner is ready."

"But I want to see Graham ask Rose to dinner," Alice whined. "It is the most exciting thing that has happened in days, aside from Daniel's visits.

"You will have your own dinner invitation to look forward to if Daniel carries on as he has," Aunt Sarah assured her before closing the French doors, leaving me and Graham alone.

Graham turned to me and sighed. "Your family is very lively."

I couldn't help but laugh. "That they are. Alice most of all."

He nodded in agreement and then bit his lower lip, looking up at me beneath his pale eyebrows. Once upon a time, I had seen Achilles Prideaux in his features, but now I wondered at how I ever could have compared them. Graham was open and wide—large eyes, broad mouth, welcoming smile. Achilles had an air of mystery around him at all times, standing in the corners with his slanted eyes and angular chin. Thin mustache aside, they were different in almost every way.

"I suppose my next question will not be a surprise to you," Graham said, tipping his head to the sitting room where Alice and Aunt Sarah were talking very loudly about the weather. "I know it is short notice, but would you like to accompany me to dinner?"

"I will have to ask Aunt Sarah, as I know the servants have been preparing dinner, and—"

"You may go," Aunt Sarah called through the door. "It will be no inconvenience to me. You eat like a bird. Barely enough to make a difference."

My face flushed, embarrassed. No matter how unwise it might be to accept his invitation while still unsure of my feelings, it seemed better than denying him and having to explain my hesitance to Alice and Aunt Sarah.

"Allow me ten minutes to change," I said, clutching the bouquet to my chest and backing towards the stairs.

Graham smiled wider than I'd ever seen and nodded. "I'll wait here."

A LIVE BAND played jazz music on a stage in the corner and every table was occupied by a young couple, usually holding hands and whispering to one another. The restaurant we'd eaten at our first night in the city with Aunt Sarah had drawn the old-money crowd, but this place catered to the young.

"I don't usually frequent places like this," Graham said, leaning across the table. He seemed nervous in the setting, though not uncomfortable. He glanced around with wide eyes like he wanted to see and remember everything.

"It seems very popular," I agreed, unable to stop myself from comparing the riotous couples around us with the quiet dignitaries that frequented The White Tiger Club. A line formed between Graham's brows, and I rushed to clarify. "Very fun. I'm enjoying the change in pace."

He let out a sigh of relief. "I'm glad. I thought we could both use a little fun. With everything that has happened the last few weeks, I almost forgot we are young."

"Oh?"

"Yes," he said, sliding his chair closer to mine so we were sitting on the same side of the table facing the stage. "You stayed with the Hutchins' in Simla, and nothing against their kindness, but they are hardly in their prime. Mr. Hutchins spent every second working and Mrs. Hutchins scarcely left the bungalow. And all of my companions for the last several years have been military men."

"Aren't you yourself a military man?" I teased.

"In the same way you are a British official's daughter," he said with a smirk.

I pulled back, suddenly on guard. "What is that supposed to mean?"

Graham's smile told me it was an innocent comment made in passing, but something about it felt ominous. Could he be making a crude comment on the fact that my father—or the man he believed to be my father—was dead, meaning I was no longer an official's daughter? Or was he choosing this public location to inform me that he knew I was not truly Mr. Beckingham's daughter? Both seemed outlandish, but otherwise, I could not puzzle out the meaning of the strange phrase.

Graham seemed to note the change in my tone, and he reached out, placing his hand over mine. "I only meant that you are unlike the other women in your same position. I hope you did not think I meant to insult you."

I softened slightly, both with relief and apology. "It would only be an insult if you liked the other women in my position you've met."

His smirk returned. "Not half as much as I like you, my dear Rose."

I looked away, finding his attention too fixed on my face. "You are too kind a man to truly feel that way about your female friends in India."

He shook his head. "My feelings have nothing to do with their faults and everything to do with your virtues."

"Virtues," I said, dismissing the word with a wave. "Since when is causing trouble a virtue?"

"Modesty." Graham lifted a finger as if he was going to count off my admirable traits one by one. He held up a second finger.

"Truly, Graham, I have you fooled." I looked around the room in hopes of catching a waiter. We'd been sitting down for ten minutes and had yet to see anyone about ordering our food.

"No, you have me enchanted, Rose Beckingham."

My skin was suddenly damp with nervous sweat. I felt like I'd been backed into a corner though we were in the middle of the room. I felt trapped. This feeling was not helped when Graham slid his chair even closer to mine until his knee nearly touched mine.

"I've been enchanted since the day I first met you in front of The Hutchins' bungalow. You were exciting and beautiful, so unlike anyone I'd ever known. You are always searching and prying, ill-content to leave things as they are. Instead, you see them as you wish they were."

His opinion of me was obviously colored by the relative newness of his affections, otherwise he would have seen me as the woman who risked his reputation several times in order to selfishly gather information. He would see me as a nosy girl who fancied herself a detective despite no proper training as such.

"You make the mundane extraordinary, and I fear you have forever ruined any chances of me enjoying a normal life," Graham continued, having no idea how each of his words clung to me like anchors, pulling me below the surface until I could not breathe. "Before meeting you, I never would have packed up on one day's notice and sailed across the ocean. I never would have taken leave from my duties and travelled to New York on a whim. But Rose, you make me want to do extraordinary things. You make me want to be an extraordinary man."

The faster Graham spoke, the faster my eyes darted around the room. I needed someone, anyone to offer me the smallest excuse to end this conversation. I liked Graham. Truly. But in what way? I was not sure. He had been a good, true friend to me, and I appreciated the steadfastness of his concern, but did that mean I wanted him to fawn over me the way Charles fawned over

Catherine? Did that mean I wanted to flush every time he walked into the room and be introduced as his date at every social function we attended? I could not see myself playing the role of the dutiful partner that, no matter how much Graham protested, I knew he truly wanted. Even if I did feel the same way about Graham—which I was not certain was true—returning his affections now felt like a betrayal because I knew he had no real understanding of exactly how different I was from other women.

My heart beat wildly in my chest, and I scanned the crowd again, seeing without really seeing anything until I saw *him* and froze. Graham's voice faded to nothing in my ears, and everyone else in the room seemed to fall into darkness. Only Achilles Prideaux was illuminated.

He moved around the edge of the room, navigating around tables and chairs, but when he reached a door set into the back wall, he looked up, his gaze falling at once on me, and I knew this was it. He had the information and had come to deliver it. I stood up before I realized I would need to make an excuse to Graham.

His mouth was hanging open like he'd been in the middle of saying something, and I'd interrupted him. Which I felt certain I had. I smiled. "I'm sorry. I need to use the ladies' room."

He blinked a few times, bewildered, and then dutifully stood and bowed, excusing me.

I rushed from the table like I'd just been freed from a burning building, and as if the restaurant had been brimming with acrid smoke, I didn't take a gasping breath until I'd walked through the door I'd seen Achilles move through and followed the hallway and another door to a narrow alley between two brick buildings.

Evening air filled my lungs, and I was surprised at how clammy my skin had become sitting at the table.

"I see you got my message."

I turned to see Achilles leaning against the brick wall and spinning his cane in front of him. When I approached, he pressed the cane into the ground and stood tall, towering over me. I'd forgotten how tall he was during my time away.

"Very subtle." I rolled my eyes. "Was this truly the most opportune moment? You may not have noticed, but I was in the middle of dinner."

"No, I noticed," he said, dark eyebrow raising. "From my vantage point, it appeared you were eager for an exit. I simply obliged."

I was grateful for the darkness when my cheeks flushed. Achilles had noticed from across the room what Graham had failed to see sitting next to me.

"I only have a minute," I continued. "My date is waiting inside."

Achilles removed a small piece of paper from an inside jacket pocket and handed it to me. It was a list of names.

"Shorter than I anticipated," I said, counting only thirty names in total.

"It is not exhaustive," he said curtly, annoyed at my displeasure. "I can retrieve more, but these seemed to be the most pertinent. Though you told me nothing of what you are investigating, I assumed you would be most interested in the names that had connections to both England

and India. If I was mistaken, then forgive me, and I'll take the list and try again."

He reached for the paper, but I pulled it out of his grip. "I do not believe you are mistaken."

I scanned the list just as I had scanned the faces inside the restaurant moments before, seeing but not seeing, hoping for a name to jump out at me. One did: William Alexander Beckingham. However, that was information I already knew and the reason I'd asked for the list in the first place, so I continued on until my eyes stumbled over Charles Cresswell's name only two lines down.

"Who is your male friend?"

I pressed my finger to Charles' name, annoyed at having been interrupted, and looked up at Achilles. "Excuse me?"

He looked down the alley as if he didn't care, dark brows pinched together. "You called your dinner a date. I only wonder how you know the man."

"I suspect you know the man already," I said. I had underestimated Achilles on several occasions, but never again. He always knew more than he let on. It was what made him a world-class detective.

His cane tapped a quick rhythm on the ground. "After so much time spent together on the ship from Bombay, I would have thought you'd be tired of one another. In my experience, you tire quickly with the company of friends."

Clearly, I had wounded Achilles more deeply than I understood when I left him in Morocco. However, unlike Graham's feelings, I had every confidence Achilles' would recover from my rebuff. "Graham is more persistent than most of my friends."

Achilles looked at me from the corner of his eye. "And is that a quality you admire?"

I shrugged and told him the truth. "The answer to that question has yet to be revealed even to me."

He seemed satisfied enough with this answer, and I returned to the list, skimming past the next four letters in the alphabet without recognizing another name. And then, I nearly dropped the list.

"What is it?" Achilles asked, noting the change in my demeanor and moving forward.

I read the name again and again, feeling the connections being forged in my mind.

"Do you recognize a name?" Achilles asked.

General Thomas Hughes. The same man who had supposedly hung himself from the rafters of the White Tiger Club's library just prior to my arrival in the city. I now knew his death to have been a murder carried out by the same man who threw the bomb through the Beckingham's car window. Mr. Barlow had admitted to killing the General and to being part of an organized ring of international assassins who were targeting British diplomats. He had told me all of this with the intention of killing me first, but I managed to end his life, thus sparing my own.

What I had not known, however, was General Hughes' connection to the Paris Peace Conference, and therefore, his connection to Mr. Beckingham. The two men had not only been diplomats living in Simla during the time of their deaths, but diplomats who had both had a hand in settling affairs after the war.

"Rose?" Achilles leaned forward, catching my eye and bringing my gaze up to his face. "You have gone pale."

I shook my head. "I lost myself in thought."

His eyes narrowed. He did not trust me, as he had every right not to. "Will you be needing a more extensive list, or will this one do?"

"This will do," I said, tucking the piece of paper into my silk handbag and pulling the strings tight to close it. "Thank you for your assistance."

Achilles sighed. "So, is this the end of our communication, or will you require my help again?"

"Not at the moment. I have no doubt, however, that we will run into one another again."

"My time in the city is coming to an end. I'm leaving for London tomorrow," he said, glancing over at me before looking back down the alley.

"Is that an invitation to join you?" I asked with a smile.

Achilles did not return the kind gesture. He simply shook his head. "I would be a fool to ask. You do not follow anyone, Rose Beckingham. Least of all me."

I could not work out whether his comment was an insult or a compliment. "Then, are you expecting me to ask you to extend your stay in the city?"

"I can't stay," he said. "I have business waiting in London."

That was not really the answer to my question, and we both knew it. "But would you stay? If you did not have pressing business to attend to?"

I didn't know why the answer mattered to me, yet I could not stop myself from asking the question. Achilles adjusted his tie nervously and tapped his cane on the ground, the sound echoing off the brick walls. "You should return to your date before he comes searching for you. If he knows you well, he may be beginning to suspect you've run away."

"I do not run away nearly as often as you seem to think I do," I argued.

Finally, Achilles smiled, this time because he had managed to upset me, and he knew it. I could have kicked his cane out from under him. Then, his smile faltered, and he lowered his voice. "It may do no good, but I would be remiss not to warn you about your companion."

All teasing between us forgotten, I leaned forward. "You are talking about Graham Collins? You know something?"

He shook his head. "I do not know anything, no. But I find his motivations to be suspect."

The tightness in my chest relaxed. "Is that so?"

"Yes, in fact," he continued. "The man hardly knows you and yet he travelled around the world to be with you. It rings suspicious to me and it ought to catch your attention, as well."

Something was catching my attention, but it had little to do with Graham's motivations and everything to do with Achilles'. He was jealous. Quite jealous. And I found it all immensely amusing.

"Is it so suspicious that a man could enjoy my company so much?" I asked. Then I waved a hand, stopping him from speaking. "Actually, do not answer that. It is an invitation to insult."

"I would never seek to insult you," Achilles said.

"I do not believe you for a moment," I said with a smile. "You may not understand the feeling that has overcome my travelling companion, but his motivations are clear enough to me. He enjoys my company, and now I must return to him in order to determine whether I enjoy his equally as well."

It felt good to be honest with someone about Graham, even if that person was Achilles. I also felt a small amount of guilt removed from me at the sight of his obvious relief. I had not settled on a decision regarding Graham, and clearly it brought Achilles some level of comfort.

He bowed low. "I will leave you to your date, then. Sorry to intrude."

"Thank you for your help," I said again. "Until we meet again."

Achilles moved down the alley, raising his cane high into the air in lieu of a wave. "Until we meet again, Mademoiselle Beckingham."

Once Achilles disappeared around the corner, I leaned against the brick wall and closed my eyes, allowing myself thirty seconds to think.

Mr. Beckingham, General Hughes, and Charles Cresswell were all three respected men in the world of politics, and now two of them were dead. Charles' nervousness had been a mystery to me because I did not understand the shared connection between him and the dead men. But Charles had no doubt made the connection. Catherine claimed her fiancé had grown nervous a few weeks before the time of her letter, which would have been around the same time as news came out regarding General Hughes' suicide. Charles must have realized what I was only just beginning to see: someone was picking off important men from the 1919 Paris negotiations one by one.

"Rose?"

I opened my eyes and pushed away from the wall, spinning to find Graham standing in the open doorway that led into the restaurant. His eyes were wide with concern, forehead wrinkled. "Is everything all right? You were gone a long while, so I came to make sure you were not ill. Are you ill?"

I looked down the alley to be certain Achilles was not still lingering there, and then nodded. "Yes, I'm afraid I am. I have not been feeling well, and I came outside for a bit of fresh air. Sorry, I did not realize I'd been gone so long."

Graham rushed forward, placing a hand on my back. "Are you feeling better or—?"

"I should probably go home," I said, holding a hand to my stomach and offering an apologetic smile. "I am sorry to ruin the dinner you planned."

"I am sorry you do not feel well," Graham said, leading me down the alley and around the block to the front of the restaurant where we would meet the driver.

During the drive home, he spoke at length about rescheduling our dinner as soon as I felt better, and I nodded along without hearing him.

Mr. Barlow was dead now, which meant he could not

be the man hunting Charles Cresswell, but there had been other assassins working in the ring. Achilles and I had tracked one down in Tangier. How many others could there be? Charles Barlow had told me he was hired by a man called "The American" who supplied him with a list of targets, and I knew immediately I had to uncover who "The American" was if I ever wanted this to end. If I ever wanted the killings to stop.

13

The driver dropped us off in front of Aunt Sarah's home, and Graham grabbed my hand and pressed my knuckles to his lips firmly, lingering there before looking up at me. "I hope you feel better soon, dear Rose."

"Thank you," I said weakly. "A bit of rest will do me wonders, I believe."

"And please eat something," he insisted. "I know we could not stay at the restaurant, but I do think a good meal will help to rejuvenate you. Should I come in with you and tell the servants to bring something to your room?"

I shook my head. "No, you have done enough, Graham. Thank you for your kindness, but I can see myself inside."

Graham seemed uncertain, but ultimately agreed and left after placing one more kiss on the back of my hand.

He was so concerned about my wellbeing that I almost felt guilty for lying to him. Though, not guilty enough to reveal the truth. As soon as Graham turned the corner at the end of the block, I walked down the steps, through the front gate, and turned in the opposite direction.

I only knew where Charles Cresswell lived because Catherine had provided me with the address should it prove useful in my investigating. Since Catherine had asked me to investigate covertly, I had not intended to use the address, but now seemed the right time to involve Charles in my investigation.

MR. CRESSWELL barely managed to hide his shock when a servant girl fetched him, and he found me standing in his entryway.

"Miss Beckingham," he said, a question in his tone. "Is everything all right?"

"Perfectly," I said with a smile. "I'm sorry if I've interrupted something. I know I've shown up unannounced."

Charles blinked and shook his head, seeming to remember his manners. "I'm sorry. That is no way to greet a guest. Of course you have not interrupted anything. I'm always pleased to welcome family into my home. Because we are soon to be family, after all."

He placed a special kind of emphasis on *family*, and I wondered whether he wasn't concerned my impromptu visit had something to do with what would be completely inappropriate feelings towards him.

"I'm pleased to know you feel that way. Catherine is a dear friend to me, as well as a cousin, and it is lovely to see she has found a man who appreciates her family as well as he appreciates her."

Charles smiled at the mention of Catherine. "She is a wonderful woman. I count myself lucky to know her and anyone who loves her is an immediate friend to me."

"Then may this friend request a word with you?" I asked, still smiling. "Privately."

Charles hesitated. I could not blame him. I had hardly spoken to him since my arrival in the city, and suddenly I was standing in his entrance hall asking for him to invite me inside. It was all very unusual, though necessary.

Finally, he stepped aside, gesturing for me to move into the sitting room. "Of course. Let me ask for some tea to be sent in. Should I send for Catherine, as well? She has been anxious for the two of us to get to know one another since you arrived in the city, and I'm sure she'd be pleased to know you have come here."

Charles Cresswell was an intelligent man. I could see him studying me, weighing my reaction to his suggestion. If I panicked and insisted he not invite Catherine, he would know I had come for some nefarious purpose. If I agreed and said Catherine could come, he would be immensely more comfortable and know I was a true friend to my cousin and, therefore, to him. I chose the third option.

"While I would love for my cousin to join us, I do believe the matter we will be discussing requires as few ears as possible."

Charles' eyes narrowed, but he tipped his head for me to sit and then turned to speak to the same servant who had answered the door. She dipped in a quick curtsy and then hurried off to the kitchen to make tea. When he returned to the room, he took the chair opposite me and positioned himself on the very edge as though he planned to stand up and leave shortly.

"You've caught my attention, Miss Beckingham," he said, the kindness from a moment before gone from his voice. "What could be so urgent that it required such a late visit?"

"Please, call me Rose," I said. "And once again, I am sorry to intrude, but I wanted to ensure I could speak to you alone."

"As you've said." Charles folded his hands one on top of the other on his knee. "We do not know one another well, so I am curious what we could have to discuss that would require secrecy."

"Were you familiar with my father, Charles?"

He weighed each of my words carefully before responding. "Not personally, no. We shared acquaintances, as I told Catherine."

"What of General Thomas Hughes?"

The question caught him by surprise, which was obvious in the raise of his brows and the parting of his lips. "I do not understand your line of questioning, Miss Beckingham."

"Rose," I reminded him. "And this is not meant to be an interrogation. I only wish to know how many acquaintances we share."

"You knew General Hughes?" he asked.

"Unfortunately, no," I said sadly. "I did not have the pleasure of meeting him before..."

Charles' eyes went wide, and he shot to his feet. "I shall send for Catherine. She would be distraught to know she missed the opportunity to talk just the three of us."

"If Catherine arrives, we will not be able to talk," I said, leveling my gaze at him.

Charles met my eyes and held my stare for several seconds before dropping down into his chair as though exhausted and running a hand through his gray-speckled hair. "What is it you know, Rose? I hardly know you, yet it is obvious you know something about me. I beg you to make it clear and save me the speculation."

I considered how to address the matter for a moment before settling on what I believed would secure the best outcome. "Catherine sent for me."

At the mention of his fiancé, Charles' eyebrows pinched. "She sent you here?"

I shook my head. "Not here exactly, but she requested I come from India to meet you."

"Whatever for?" he asked, voice slightly frantic. "Is she having second thoughts about our marriage? Did she need you to come and confirm we are a good match? If so, I apologize for treating you harshly, it is just that—"

The man was spiraling, which meant I had landed my blow perfectly. Charles struck me as a strong confident man, but if he had any weakness, it was Catherine.

"Her only doubts stem from your sudden nervousness," I admitted. "Catherine noted a change in your behavior, and it worried her enough that she wanted me to come and help her uncover what was wrong."

Charles sagged between his shoulder blades, face in

his hands. His voice came out muffled between his fingers. "I cannot believe I worried her to that extent. I did my best to keep her separate from my troubles."

"She loves you, Charles. Your troubles are her troubles. You are a bright man. Surely you know that."

He looked up at me, and I could see the exhaustion in every line of his face, in the downturned angle of his eyes. "My troubles are a burden too large for her to bear. It is unfair of me to place it on her. I thought, perhaps, I could solve the problem myself, but I am beginning to think that impossible."

"What is the burden?" I asked. "I have plenty of my own and have no qualms about taking on yours, as well."

He shook his head. "I cannot say. Please do not ask again."

"Charles," I started. "Consider the questions I have asked you already and—"

The servant, a young woman not much older than Alice, came in carrying a tray of tea. She set it down carefully on the table between us, and I could tell she was keenly aware that she had interrupted our conversation. She stood back and folded her hands behind her back. "Can I get you anything else, Mr. Cresswell?"

"That will be all, Francis. Thank you," he said with a wave.

The girl, clearly attuned to the secretive nature of our conversation if not the content, closed the doors behind her.

"Consider the questions I have asked you already," I repeated. "If it is not clear to you that I have a suspicion as to what may be causing your troubles, then perhaps your troubles are not what I thought."

Charles paused to study me, and I could tell he was weighing not only whether to lay his burdens on me, but whether he could trust me with them. I was Catherine's cousin, but we hardly knew one another, and I suspected he had good reason to be suspicious of most people.

After a few moments, he leaned forward, eyes settled on my face, and spoke quietly. "I know it may be difficult to believe, but I have reason to suspect I am the next target of an assassin."

"And I know it may be difficult for you to believe," I repeated, leaning forward, as well, "but I believe you wholeheartedly."

"You do not know me well enough to believe me on trust alone," he said, standing up and pacing towards the fireplace. "Which means you must have proof."

"I was right. You are a bright man."

"What do you know?" Charles asked wearily.

"You never answered my question before. About General Thomas Hughes."

"I know him," Charles said before correcting himself. "Or, I knew him, I suppose. He died a few weeks ago."

I nodded. "Did you hear of the circumstances surrounding his death?"

"Suicide," Charles said. "Though many who knew him have their doubts."

"As they should," I said. "I have it on good authority that General Hughes was murdered."

Charles' eyes narrowed. "Who told you this?"

"The killer," I said without flinching. "The same man who murdered my father and mother."

"You spoke with the killer?" Charles asked, taking a step forward. "When?"

"Before I killed him."

Charles opened his mouth and closed it several times before shaking his head and falling onto the end of the sofa where I was sitting. "Did the man reveal his motives?"

I shook my head.

"And you really killed him?" he asked, expression cautious yet hopeful.

"I did," I admitted. "Though, I would appreciate your discretion in the matter. It is not a secret, but word spreads, and I would hate for opinions of me to be colored."

Charles nodded in understanding and let his eyes flutter closed, his hands clapped in a kind of praying position in front of him. "So, it is really over."

Suddenly, I understood the look on his face and the tone of his questions. Charles thought I had killed the one and only assassin. He believed his paranoia for the last several weeks had been for nothing. And I had to tell him otherwise.

"Well, in fact," I said softly. "I believe there may be another assassin."

He snapped his attention to me. "Another?"

I shrugged. "Several more, actually. I can't be sure. Before I killed him, the last assassin told me that he received a list of targets from a man calling himself 'The American.'"

"The American," Charles repeated, his voice cracking. "As in, he lives in America?"

"That is what I was led to believe," I said. "I don't know any more than that."

Charles rocked back and forth several times before standing up and pacing once again across the floor, fists wringing at his sides. "I am a good man. An honorable man. I've done my best to serve my country and the world. To look after the interests of those who could not help themselves. How am I deserving of this?"

I crossed the room quickly and laid a hand on Charles' shoulder. He shrugged it off but stopped pacing and faced me. "We do not know for certain that you are a target. You are right to be on high alert, but many people were at the conference, and—"

"I had the ear of the Prime Minister. If these murders are connected with that conference then my name is certainly on an assassin's list somewhere," he said. Then, he dug into his pocket and pulled out a crisp white piece of paper folded down the center. "And I recently received this."

I plucked the note from his fingers. Written in an angular, tight script was a short message: *You are a fitting sacrifice for my better world.*

"A fitting sacrifice." I repeated the words under my breath, committing the letter to memory.

Charles took it back and tucked it away in his jacket. "I do not believe this note can be misinterpreted."

I couldn't disagree with him, though I wished I could. I wanted to comfort him. I wanted to convince him he had nothing to worry about, but I could not. Mr.

Beckingham had been murdered with a bomb in a public square. General Hughes had been hung from the rafter of a private club. The assassins were skilled at blending in and ingratiating themselves with their targets, but they were also prepared for random, violent attacks regardless of the bloodshed. Even with advance notice, there was every chance Charles could still be murdered.

Charles went pale and slouched back into the sofa, his hand running down his face. "Part of me thought I was paranoid. Part of me hoped I had connected two random accidents and made something larger out of it. But I was right. Someone is coming for me. And that confirmation does nothing but make me more terrified."

"I'm sorry," I said. "I wish I could say something to help. All I can tell you is that I am doing my best to track down 'The American,' and when I do, I will know how many assassins there are."

"Why don't we ask the police?" Charles asked, sitting up suddenly.

"A friend of mine alerted the authorities in Tangier, but nothing was done. And I tried to explain the true circumstances of General Hughes' death to the authorities in Simla, but they refused to see it as anything but a suicide. We have no proof and the police would have nothing to base an investigation on. It is a waste of time."

"There has to be something we can do," he muttered.

"Stay safe," I said, placing a hand on his shoulder. "Be vigilant and give me time to solve this case."

When his eyes met mine, they were not exactly brimming with confidence. He looked like an animal being led to slaughter. "And you will keep me updated on your progress?"

I nodded. "Of course. You will be the first to know if I find anything."

"Thank you," he said, sighing and slouching forward. He looked utterly crestfallen, and I hated to leave him alone.

"Won't you tell Catherine any of this?" I asked.

Suddenly, he was sitting bolt upright, his eyes wide. "You can't breathe a word of this to Catherine. You can't. Promise me, Rose."

He reached out and grabbed my hand, squeezing it hard in his fingers. It was not a threat, but a plea.

"She loves you, Charles. Her past has been tumultuous. I'm sure she has told you about her brother and his crimes. She can handle this."

"But she should not have to," he said. "Besides, you of all people should know how dangerous this kind of information can be. Knowing anything about this puts her at risk, and I won't allow that. Swear to me, Rose. Swear this conversation will not leave this room."

I had come to New York City to assist Catherine, and now I would have to lie to her. I did not enjoy the prospect, but I also could not discount the truth of Charles' claims. Knowing anything about "The American" and his ring of assassins was dangerous, and the less Catherine knew, the safer she would be.

"I swear it," I said. "She will not hear a word of it from me."

Charles inhaled deeply and released the breath

slowly, nodding the entire time. "Thank you, Rose. Thank you."

He showed me to the door in silence, neither of us having any idea what to say. Idle chit chat hardly seemed appropriate after a conversation of that magnitude. So, Charles tipped his head as I stepped onto the doorstep.

"Thank you for coming, Rose."

I nodded back. "When we speak again, I hope it will be about better news."

"I hope so, too." He smiled, his eyes and mouth crinkling at the corners, and then closed the door.

Knowing the connection between General Hughes, Mr. Beckingham, and Charles Cresswell was an answer that only invited more questions. Who was orchestrating the killings? And now that Mr. Barlow was dead, was there yet another assassin we would have to contend with?

As I walked down the sidewalk, the moon offering a faint amount of light by which to see, I felt a prickling down my spine as though I was being watched. Thoughts of assassins and "The American" left my head as I focused in on my immediate surroundings. I'd walked several blocks in deep thought, paying little attention to those around me or where I was going, but now I heard every footfall against the ground, every rustle in the landscaping. I looked back over my shoulder and saw no one behind me. A couple was walking on the opposite side of the street, but they turned the corner, leaving me once again alone.

I continued on, every sense attuned to the world around

me, and though I did not hear or see anyone, I could not rid myself of the feeling that I was being followed. The longer I walked without incident, however, the more I began to suspect I had fallen victim to paranoia. My conversation with Charles about assassins and staying vigilant had clearly unnerved me, and the feeling would subside as soon as I reached Aunt Sarah's home, which was at the end of the next block. I hastened my pace, passing quickly in front of the large stone home next door, so I could finally move through the gates that had become familiar to me over the last few days and be put at ease. When I pushed the gate open was when I heard the footsteps.

They came from behind, slapping against the ground as though running, and every instinct in my body told me to run. Instead, I grabbed the blade I had taken to stashing inside of my handbag and spun around, prepared to fight.

Graham's eyes widened at the sight, and he slid to a stop.

"Graham?" I took a step backwards without lowering my weapon.

He focused on the blade and backed away, as well.

14

"Are you going to stab me, Rose?" Graham asked solemnly.

I lowered the blade to my side, my knuckles aching from my crushing grip around the handle. "Were you following me?"

"I was," Graham admitted, shifting from one foot to another, his two-toned oxfords slapping against the ground. I wondered how I had not heard him behind me.

"Would you care to explain why?" I felt exposed, but also betrayed. Yes, I had lied to him, and I was certain I would be answering for that soon enough, but following me without my knowledge was an invasion of my privacy. Even though I had lied, I deserved an explanation.

"Because you lied to me," he said simply, never once taking his eyes from my face. "I knew you were lying to me, and I wanted to know why."

"You knew?" I asked.

He nodded. "The moment I found you in the alley, I knew something had happened that you were not telling me. I have not spent so much time with you without paying attention, Rose. You may think me a silly man, but—"

"I have thought no such thing." It was only a partial lie. I believed Graham to be an intelligent man, if slightly too optimistic and prone to fits of romance.

"Regardless," he continued. "I knew you were lying to me, and when you refused to allow me to show you inside your aunt's home, I wondered if it was not because you had business elsewhere. So, I waited around the block and followed you when you set out."

"You could have come to me," I said. "You could have asked me why I had lied."

"And would you have told me you were going to visit Charles Cresswell? If I had stopped you with no knowledge of your destination, would you have revealed that truth to me?"

My face flushed in embarrassment and shame, and Graham finally looked away, too upset to look at me. I would not have told him the truth, and suggesting otherwise felt like another betrayal.

"Does Catherine know you visited her fiancé tonight?" he asked.

"No one knows," I said. "Save for myself, you, and Charles."

He nodded and kicked the toe of his shoe against the ground. "And would Catherine be disturbed to know the nature of your visit?"

My eyes widened in surprise and my hand flew to my chest. "If you are suggesting that my relationship with

Charles is anything other than friendly, I must tell you my honor is wounded."

Graham looked at me, hope flickering in his eyes. "Believe me, suspecting you of any kind of illicit relationship, especially with a man you will soon call family, wounds me in more ways than I can say. But what am I meant to think? You left our dinner under false pretenses so you could go and see him. There are not many excuses for that kind of behavior."

I slipped my blade into my purse and stepped forward to look into Graham's eyes. Though I had lied to him and given him reason to doubt me, I wanted him to know I truly meant what I said. "You told me tonight at dinner that I am unlike other women."

He nodded and looked down at the ground, embarrassed by the romantic confessions he had made to me only a couple of hours before.

"Then is it possible my motives could be unlike other women's motives? That my reasons could be unlike those of ordinary people?" I asked, reaching out for his hand.

Graham looked at my hand, considered it for a moment, and then wrapped his fingers around mine. He slouched in a mixture of relief and shame. "It is possible, Rose. Of course, it is. I should have given you the opportunity to explain before making an accusation."

"And I should not have lied," I said. Though I knew, given the chance, the only change I would have made was waiting longer to set out for Charles' home so Graham would not have followed me. Though I felt bad to have wounded him or given him reason to doubt me, I also had my reasons for being secretive. A man's life was at stake, and I would not risk his safety or my own in order to spare Graham Collins' feelings.

"Why did you?" he asked, grabbing my other hand and pressing my palms together, his hands wrapped around mine like a cage.

"I did not come to New York simply to celebrate the impending marriage of my cousin," I admitted. "I also came to help her in solving a mystery."

Graham's brow furrowed. "What kind of mystery?"

"Would you be angry if I told you it was confidential?" I asked.

He slowly released my hands, letting his own fall to his sides. "You do not trust me?"

"Of course, I trust you," I said quickly. "You have proven yourself to be a loyal friend to me, Graham. It is just that I do not want to prove myself disloyal to my cousin. She asked me to keep my investigation a secret, and that is what I've tried to do. It is why I lied to you at the restaurant. I did not feel ill; I was simply over-whelmed by the information I'd gathered and needed time to think. On the drive home, I realized I needed to speak to Charles immediately."

"And you swear there was nothing else to it other than that?" he asked. "Besides a sense of obligation to your cousin and a drive to uncover the next clue?"

"I swear it," I said, aware that it was the second time I'd been asked to swear that evening.

Graham stared at me for a moment before his thin mouth turned up in a smile. "Okay, then."

He walked me through the gates of Aunt Sarah's house and up the short path that led to the stone steps.

When we were standing on the topmost stair, he turned to me and clutched my hands.

"A loyal friend," he said.

I tilted my head to the side. "Sorry?"

"Is that how you see me?" he asked. "As a loyal friend?"

"Oh." I shifted uncomfortably, realizing the conversation had once again been steered towards the matter of our relationship, and I was no more prepared to give Graham an answer than I had been at the restaurant.

"Because I hope I have become more to you than that," he continued without waiting for my response. "As you have become much more than a friend to me. As I said at the restaurant earlier this evening, I'm not sure my life will ever be the same after knowing you. I don't see how it could be. I told you that you are an unusual woman, and tonight has only proven that. You are unusually loyal, unusually perceptive, and unusually beautiful."

Nervously, my hand lifted to my left cheek, to the scar there. I'd done it unconsciously, more a nervous habit than anything else, but Graham noticed. As he had noticed my uneasiness at the restaurant. His hand followed mine, and he curled his finger and brushed his knuckle across my cheekbone, following the dent left there by the shrapnel.

"And unusually brave," he said softly, giving me a sad smile. "You have been through so much and despite every obstacle, you have taken care of yourself. But I want you to know, Rose, that I would love to be a helper to you. I want you to know that you can trust me with your secrets and all of your other motivations. You are a remarkable woman, and I would never wish to hinder you in that regard, but I would count it an honor to be considered amongst those you trust."

"I do trust you," I interrupted. It was the simplest, most honest thing I could say.

He smiled. "Thank you."

I thought the conversation was over. I thought Graham had said what he needed to say and was going to allow me to go inside, but when I attempted to pull my hand from his grip, he clung even tighter. When I looked back at him, he was bending to one knee.

It took me several seconds to understand the image. Graham, kneeling on the ground, looking up at me with a glazed look in his eyes, a ring box open in his hand. His blonde mustache was a slash across his face, highlighting the bend of his smile.

"We have only known one another a short time, but in that time, I have become certain of one thing, Rose Beckingham: I love you. I have turned my life upside down to be near you, and I do not have a single regret. I would travel across any ocean or continent to be the man lucky enough to be by your side. However, I do hope you will make it easy on me and promise to remain by my side, as well, by becoming my wife. My dear Rose, will you marry me?"

The scene was so like and unlike anything I ever would have imagined. Here was a well-dressed, respectable, handsome man begging for me to marry him. The old me—Nellie Dennet—longed for nothing more. But now? What did Rose Beckingham want? A simple life with a respectable, handsome husband?

Suddenly, a shaft of light cut across Graham's face and then someone screamed.

I turned to see Alice standing in the doorway, her hands over her mouth, eyes wide. "Rose is getting married!"

There was a commotion behind her, and before I could say anything or move, Aunt Sarah and Catherine had joined her. Catherine's mouth was hanging open in shock and Aunt Sarah had tears welling in her eyes.

"Rose?" Catherine asked, turning to me. "What is going on?"

"Graham proposed, clearly," Alice said with a roll of her eyes.

Graham stood up, his cheeks burning a vibrant shade of red, and closed the box.

The snap of the jewelry box lid seemed to wake me up as if from a dream. I startled and then pulled my hand out of his and clapped mine together. "Well, I think we should continue this conversation another time."

Graham's mouth opened to argue, but I was already shoving my way through the door, pushing on my cousins and aunt until they were forced back into the entrance hall. When I turned to shut the door, Graham's face had fallen, his happiness given way to confusion, but I did not have the emotional energy left to feel sorry for him. Instead, I smiled, waved, and closed the door firmly.

lice skipped around the entrance hall like a child on Christmas morning. "We could hold a double wedding in Somerset. Catherine, would you mind sharing your day with Rose? It would be very convenient and the social event of the entire season."

"She didn't even say 'yes,'" Catherine snapped, stalking towards me, her evening robe cinched around her waist. "Why didn't you say 'yes'?"

"Girls," Aunt Sarah cautioned, though no one seemed to be listening to her. "I don't know that Rose's love life is any of our business. We already interrupted her proposal. It was a proposal, wasn't it, dear? That Graham Collins is so handsome and romantic. I had a servant put the flowers he brought you in a vase next to your bed. Such a gentleman."

"What are you going to say?" Alice asked, wrapping her arm through mine and pulling me towards the sitting room.

I felt like a bit of food being picked at by birds, ripped

and pulled in every direction. I yanked my arm free and moved towards the stairs. "I think I'm going to go to bed."

"You can't!" Alice cried at the same time Catherine, shouted, "No."

I sighed. "I don't have any satisfying answers for you."

"Are you going to marry him?" Alice asked, her eyes dreamy.

"I don't know," I said honestly. I had too many secrets to add yet another to my plate.

"Do you love him?" Catherine asked. Her eyes held something deeper; a warning, perhaps? She knew what loving someone meant. Clearly, she loved Charles, and knowing Catherine, she would not approve if I settled for anything less. Not because she was the romantic type, but because she believed her way was the best way regardless.

"I don't know," I repeated, feeling suddenly exhausted. My knees quaked, and I wanted to sit down on the stairs.

"He is handsome," Alice said, clinging to the stair railing with both hands and swinging back and forth. "And kind."

"He travelled all this way to protect you," Catherine said grudgingly, eyebrows furrowed like she was trying to think of something negative to say, as well.

Aunt Sarah nodded in agreement. "And he is enamored with you, my girl. He looks at you the way Charles looks at Catherine."

Catherine sneered at her aunt, annoyed with her relationship being compared to mine, and then turned to me. "He does seem to care for you."

"Thank you all for your help, but I'm going to go to bed," I said quickly, turning and mounting the stairs before they could argue. "I will talk with you more in the morning."

From the moment I slid beneath my blankets until dawn when I placed my feet on the floor, my mind raced. My thoughts reeled with possibilities for my own life and Charles Cresswell's. Suspects and wedding dress designs mingled together in my mind until I dreamt Charles Cresswell was wearing a white gown and attempting to murder Catherine.

My feelings were jumbled, and when I dressed in a light gray walking suit and slipped from the house before anyone else woke up, it was the only decision I was certain of.

I could not face my cousins and Aunt Sarah over breakfast. I could not discuss something I had not yet puzzled out in my own mind. And I could not stay at the house and wait for Graham to appear and ask the question again. Because the next time I spoke to him, I wanted to know my own heart. I wanted to be certain of my feelings and the response I would give him.

As I walked past the luxurious homes that lined Fifth Avenue, I heard a distant horn. It could have been a car or a ship, and I wondered if Achilles was on his ship yet. If he had set sail for England to leave New York behind. I wanted to see him. Achilles had a way of seeing the world that made things clear. He could probably even reveal my own feelings to me. Though, he had already made clear his opinion of Graham. The last time we'd spoken, he had warned me to be careful of him. I knew the warning stemmed from jealousy, but I couldn't help but wonder if there wasn't some truth to it. Could I be with a man who was willing to throw away his own life in order to be with me? Could I ever return the affections of someone who clearly cared for me so much? Achilles would never turn his back on his career in order to be with me or any other woman, proven by the fact that he'd told me he couldn't stay in the city due to work. Even if I'd asked him to stay, he would have gone, and I could entirely understand the impulse. I understood Achilles. I did not understand Graham.

Honestly, I did not understand men at all. Not when it came to romance. Living in an orphanage as a young girl limited my access to suitors, and when I became Rose Beckingham's companion, I spent my time accompanying her and preparing her hair and dress for dances and dinners and social functions. Rarely was I allowed to attend, and if I was, my instruction was to not leave Rose's side. There had been a few boys who had dared come close to me, but Rose usually persuaded them to look her direction, and I never much minded.

I much preferred a mystery to romance. I felt more comfortable sneaking through dark rooms than I did on the dance floor. I would rather be eavesdropping on conversations than attempting to carry one. However, I was reaching an age where people would begin to question an unmarried woman. I had Rose's inheritance to sustain me, but I would be a spinster soon enough, whispered about and mocked. Would I rather be an outcast able to solve crimes or a member of society playing the role of a dainty, dutiful wife?

The questions plagued me with no answers in sight, so I turned my mind to the investigation, focusing my energy on a puzzle I might be able to solve.

General Hughes, Mr. Beckingham, and Charles Cresswell had all been active participants at the Paris Peace Conference in 1919, and now two of the three had been killed by assassins, and according to the note Charles received, he was the next target.

You are a fitting sacrifice for my better world.

Whose better world? Who would consider the world a better place if the people responsible for creating peace were dead?

I slowed my pace, the beginnings of an idea forming in my mind. Someone for whom peace was not achieved. Someone who viewed the Treaty of Versailles as a weak attempt at justice. Someone who had lost something in the war far greater than money. Someone with the power and position to command assassins.

Suddenly, I heard his voice in my head. *We all have to be willing to sacrifice in order to create the world we want. Do you understand?*

I stopped walking entirely, frozen in the middle of the sidewalk. Albion Rooker. The man I had met my second night in the city. The man who, during our first and only interaction, admitted to me that he was upset about the outcome of the conference and worried people were forgetting his sons who died in the war. Could he be "The American" commanding assassins to commit these murders?

The idea had come to me so suddenly and seemed such a simple solution that I almost couldn't trust myself.

Was this a theory born from desperation and lack of sleep or did it hold merit? There was only one way to be certain.

Already on Fifth Avenue, I was standing in front of Albion Rooker's extravagant home in a matter of minutes.

Albion's house was made of the same polished stone as Aunt Sarah's, but where her windows were thrown wide, making the home look open and welcoming, Albion's windows were all drawn. It was early in the day, so perhaps the servants had not opened them yet, but thinking back, they had been drawn closed even on the evening of the party. The inside of the house, packed with people, had been illuminated only with candles and fireplaces.

The house faced west, so the morning sunrise cast an ominous black shadow across the lawn. As I walked towards the front door, I shivered from the change in temperature.

I didn't have a plan for how to approach the situation. As I'd already told Charles, calling the police would solve nothing. If Albion was 'The American,' he would have connections with local police. And even if he didn't, he had the wealth and power to divert their investigation elsewhere, especially since I had no proof. So, I had to talk to him. He had revealed a great deal about himself and his feelings about the Treaty of Versailles the first night I met him, so surely a longer conversation would provide something else incriminating. Or, at least, I hoped.

The door was twice as tall as me and solid as I knocked on it, sounding more like stone than wood.

When no one answered, I knocked again, bruising my knuckles against the intricately carved door. Angels decorated the higher corners, looking down at the knocker as though in judgment, and demons lurked along the bottom of the frame, clawed hands reaching out to pull unsuspecting visitors down to the depths. Even though I knew they were only carvings, I took a step back as I waited.

The drapes on either side of the doorway were pulled closed, so I couldn't see if there was movement inside, and the door was far too solid to hear any movement on the other side. I knocked a third time, waited an appropriate length of time, and then tried the handle for myself. To my surprise, the door opened.

As children, my brother and I had broken into homes just for the excitement of it. Usually apartments we knew were vacant or where we knew the owners and had watched them leave for the day. The homes were always as rundown and bare of items of worth as our own. But Albion Rooker's home was grand. I would have been afraid to even step on his lawn as a child, and now I was slipping into his darkened entryway and closing the door behind me, twisting the handle so the latch wouldn't thud inside the frame.

The door had been unlocked, but I didn't think that had any bearing on the inappropriateness of the act. Clearly, Albion was not accepting visitors and anyone there for non-criminal purposes would have escorted themselves out. Yet, I walked in deeper.

If I ran into a servant, I planned to tell them I was out for a walk and saw the door had been left open, and I'd come inside to check that Albion was well since I knew he had been in poor health. Aunt Sarah lived close enough that it was a plausible scenario, and even if Albion had his suspicions, he would not be able to prove otherwise. However, as I moved through the dining room and the grand sitting room where the jazz band and dance floor had been assembled, I didn't see or hear another living soul. It was as if Albion's small army of servants had all taken the same day off. No matter how often I stopped and strained my ears, I didn't hear even a creak of floorboards in the entire mansion.

When I made it to the kitchen and found the room entirely devoid of light or activity, I began to settle. Clearly, no one was home.

Perhaps, Albion had retired to a country estate for a spell. Fresh air was often recommended for those in poor health, and the city offered very little of that. Maybe he'd left after his most recent party, taking his servants with him, and accidentally leaving his front door unlocked. As I continued through the first floor, seeing no sign of anyone having been in the house recently at all, this theory seemed more and more likely, and I lowered my guard.

The first floor was wide and open. The ceilings were intimidatingly tall, doorways twice the width of my arm span thrown open, allowing for easy movement throughout the mansion. It was in direct opposition to the closed off nature of the exterior of his home, so I supposed, whatever he kept hidden from the outside world was no secret within the walls of his own home.

Then, I reached a small door at the end of a narrow

hallway. I dismissed it at first, thinking it a closet or storage room, but something propelled me forward. When I pulled the door open, revealing a small room lined with shelves and a desk in the center, I realized why the room had been discretely tucked away. It was Albion's office. And, if he was indeed 'The American,' the place where I was most likely to find the evidence.

I pulled the door closed behind me, leaving it slightly ajar to avoid the sound of the latch, and moved towards the desk. The rest of the house appeared in perfect order, but the office was clearly Albion's private space, unvisited even by the servants. Papers spilled across the desk in no discernible arrangement, half-drunk cups of tea were leaving rings in the corners of the wood, and unlike the rest of the meticulously clean home, every surface was covered in dust and the signs of Albion's papery fingers moving through it as he worked.

But worked on what? He was an old, ailing man who survived on the wealth he had accumulated all his life. What work did he have left to do?

I sat down behind the desk and began filing through his papers. Letters from friends, drafts of his responses, written in a shaking hand, and documentation of wages paid and owed to the many people who helped keep his home running. I skimmed over the letters, searching for anything of use, but Albion apparently wrote of nothing more interesting than the weather and state of the stock market with his friends because they spoke of little else. If he did write to them about the imminent rise of Germany due to what he considered a lackluster punishment, his friends did not feel compelled to write on the matter in their own letters.

As I moved clockwise through his drawers, I began to worry I had broken into his home with no cause. I'd done my best to replace things on his desk where I had found them—though it was already such a mess I doubted he would notice—but the guilt of spying on a lonely, innocent old man left me feeling uneasy. Then, I reached the top right drawer in the desk. It was locked.

For a man who had so much of his business spread openly across his desk, what could be worth hiding away in a locked drawer? The keyhole was small and iron, so I set about looking for the key to open it. I searched the bookshelves on the wall behind me, running my hand along the shelves near the ceiling in hopes of finding something. I even looked inside the cold fireplace in case the key could be hidden there, but found nothing. Finally, I flopped back down into the chair, discouraged, and I heard a metallic rattle. I got up at once and turned the chair over, discovering the source of the rattle. The key was hanging from a small metal chain around the wooden crossbeam of the chair. My sitting down had rattled it against the wooden leg. I thanked the Heavens for the clue, removed the key, and eagerly unlocked the drawer.

Unlike the rest of the desk, this drawer was neat and organized. A single, short stack of papers sat in the center like someone had only just stacked them. I pulled the stack from the drawer carefully, sensing it was important. As soon as I read the first page, I knew it was.

A list of names stretched from the top to bottom,

written in an angular, neat scrawl I vaguely recognized. Over half the names had angry dark slashes through them, and it was only when I saw 'William Alexander Beckingham' scratched out that I understood what I was looking at.

A hit list.

Beneath that was Charles Cresswell's name, still unmarked. And further down, General Thomas Hughes was crossed out. Every slash was a life lost. A target eliminated.

And why would Albion Rooker have this list if he had nothing to do with their deaths? If he was nothing more than an innocent old man? He wouldn't. The list was all the proof I needed. I shuffled the stack together, planning to take it with me and peruse it in private at Aunt Sarah's house, but before I could stand up, I heard the office door latch catch in the frame.

I shot up, the pages falling from my hands and spilling across the floor, and looked up to see Albion Rooker, hunched and weak, standing in the room with me. He was smiling.

16

"Miss Beckingham," Albion said, tipping his head.

"I'm sorry," I stammered, looking at the pages cluttered around my feet. If I could grab the list of names, I could outrun the old man and keep my proof. But it was mixed in amongst the mess now. I couldn't see it. "The front door was open, and I—"

"Showed yourself in," he finished, moving towards me. "Seems an odd thing to do. We've only met once before. How strange you should feel so comfortable here."

I backed away on instinct, moving to the far corner of the desk. The man was old, but he could wield a blade the same as anyone else. I did not want him getting too close. My own fingers itched to grab the blade hidden beneath my sweater.

"It was not a sense of comfort that brought me inside, but concern," I lied. "I worried perhaps something had happened to you, and—"

"And you thought you would find the answer hidden in my desk drawers," he interrupted again, still moving forward. "Once again, strange."

"I may have become distracted." He came around the left side of the desk as I moved around the right, keeping the wooden table between us. But with every step, I moved further from the evidence I'd dropped on the floor.

Albion moved around to the back of the desk and eyed the open desk drawer and the pages I'd dropped on the floor. He moved to pick them up, and despite the desire to chance it and grab as many of the pages as I could, I moved away. There would be no sense in finding proof of his crimes if I died in the process. He clicked his tongue in annoyance. "I think I am your distraction, pulling you from your mission. You came into this home for something specific, and I suspect you found it." He looked up at me, his milky eyes narrowed. "You are lying to me."

Clearly, there was no reason to continue the charade. The man knew what I'd found. He knew what I was doing there. "Do not let it bother you, Albion. I lie to a great many people."

He stared at me for a moment and then laughed. The sound was dry and strangled, but filled with genuine amusement. "I'm sure you do."

He bent down slowly, groaning with the effort, and picked up a handful of the papers on the floor. He flipped through them silently, studying each one before throwing it down. Near the bottom of the handful, however, he separated one page from the rest, grabbed a match he had been carrying in his pocket, and struck it on the corner of the desk. Then, he lit the page on fire.

As the flames neared his fingers, he turned and dropped the page into the cold fireplace, watching as it turned to ash. Then, he turned back to me with a smile on his face.

"Why did you do that?" I asked. "What did that say?"

"If I told you, then it would ruin my fun," he said, still smiling.

Before I could respond, the old man doubled over as a wet cough tore through him. He fell forward, gripping the edge of the desk, and despite what I was coming to learn about him, my instinct was still to reach out and keep him from falling. Even knowing he could very well be the leader of a ring of international assassins, I wanted to keep the old man from collapsing.

Albion let the cough wrack through him, and then dropped down in his chair. His skin, deathly pale the first night I met him, looked almost yellow now. His eyes were bloodshot, and I could see the veins running under his skin.

"Though, my fun is already coming to an end," he said. "As I'm sure you can tell, I am dying."

"I heard you have been ill," I said.

He dismissed me with a wave of his hand. "To more important matters. Why were you snooping amongst my papers?"

"I wasn't—"

He wagged a gnarled finger at me. "Do not lie to me. We've already discussed this. I stood there at the door and watched you look through my things for almost a minute before announcing my presence."

A shiver ran down me at the realization that I had been being watched. "Why would you do that?"

He raised a gray eyebrow. "Don't ask questions you know the answer to. It's a waste of my valuable time."

"You're 'The American,'" I said clearly.

Albion nodded. "See? Isn't it much nicer when we both say what we mean?"

"Why don't you say what you mean," I said. "Why did you do this? Why did you kill so many people? My family?"

Albion bent forward, coughing into the crook of his elbow, and then leaned back on his side, breathing heavily. "If you are looking for sympathy for your loss, I will show you the same compassion your father showed me when I explained the loss of my sons."

"Mr. Beck—My father was a compassionate man," I argued.

"Was he?" Albion asked. "As a retired general, I was present during the Peace Conference. I was there to offer my wisdom, and I did just that. I advocated for harsher penalties for Germany to ensure a war on this scale would never happen again. To ensure that fine young men like my boys wouldn't die in vain. But men like your father and everyone else on that list of names you just read argued against me. They pushed aside my wisdom in favor of their own brand of diluted justice. And I swore to them then that I would not forget. And so, I haven't."

"Those men did not kill your sons. My father did not kill your sons."

"He may as well have," Albion spat. "Germany is on the rise again. You heard the men talking at my party that night. They have joined the League of Nations, and it will not be long before their bloodlust will lead us into war again. I will not be alive to see it, but mark my words."

He sounded delusional, and to do what he had done —killing off innocent men whose only crimes were trying to bring about peace—he had to be delusional. There was no other rational explanation. He coughed again, the sound clawing its way out of his throat. He was even sicker than he'd been at the party. Whatever was wrong with him, it had accelerated.

"Now," he continued, wiping his mouth. I thought I saw red splatters on the white sleeve of his shirt, but he folded his hands in his lap before I could get a good look. "What did you see amongst my papers?"

"A list of names," I admitted. "The names of men you've had murdered."

"And is that all?"

I did not want to admit that I hadn't seen anything else. I wanted to convince Albion I'd seen everything so he would admit more to me and open up about the breadth of his operation.

"Even if you don't answer, I know you didn't see anything else," he said, appraising me. "I'd be able to tell if you had. You probably would not still be standing here."

"I'm not leaving," I said. "Why would I leave when you are the man leading a ring of assassins? The man responsible for threatening my future brother-in-law?

Why would I leave when I finally found the man who was behind the murder of my family?"

His smile was mocking, and I didn't understand it. I'd caught him. He had admitted the truth to me. He should be trying to get rid of me. Or, at the very least, begging for his life.

"I didn't intend for the murder of your entire family," he said, looking contemplative, though not apologetic. "Your father was targeted because he was instrumental in swaying the decisions of the then British Prime Minister. I told the assassin to do whatever he must to ensure your father died. He, unfortunately, chose a method that caused an uncomfortable amount of press for me. And, in the case of you, was not an actual guarantee of death. He thought there was no chance of survivors. And yet..." He extended his arm in my direction like he was a ringmaster showcasing a new freak in his show.

"I don't care to hear your reasoning," I said. "I'm sending for the police."

"I would not bother," he said, leaning back in the chair like sitting up was too difficult. His head lulled to one side as if his neck could no longer support the weight. "I'll be dead before they arrive."

I crossed my arms over my chest, and I could feel the handle of my blade pressing into my skin. There was no need for it here. Albion was weak and old. "I am not planning to kill you."

"It would not matter if you were," he said. "I'll be dead all the same. I've taken measures to end my own life."

"What does that mean?" I asked, looking around the

room for any signs of a gun or explosives. Whatever Albion had planned, I did not intend to be taken down with him.

He reached into the inner pocket of his jacket and pulled out a small vial. "I drank the contents while standing on the other side of that door. If the man who sold it to me was telling the truth, I'll be dead in a matter of minutes."

I blinked several times, trying to process the information. "Why? Why would you kill yourself?"

He shrugged as if the decision had been a simple one. "I am an old man, Rose. Sickly and, if I am being honest, lonely. Even if you had not come to my home today, I planned to die. My work is nearly finished, and I am tired."

"Nearly finished?" I asked, stepping forward, eyes trained on the still unburnt stack of papers Albion had in his lap. What information did they still hold? "How many more men are going to die?"

"Perhaps, it is better this way," Albion mused as though I hadn't spoken. "It will be nice to have a witness to my death. Someone who can tell the world what happened. And why. A witness does a great deal to spread a story."

"I'm not spreading anything for you," I said, my lip curling back. "When you die, I will not utter your name again. You could have been mourned, but your actions are unforgivable. You are no longer worthy of remembering."

Albion looked up at me and smiled. "I truly do admire your tenacity, Rose Beckingham. So much so that

I almost regret I will not live long enough to rescind the order for your death."

My heart clenched in my chest, and my entire body went still. I knew I was in danger, but to hear it confirmed sent a chill through me. "How have you justified my death? I played no part in handing out punishment after the war. I was little more than a child."

"You killed my men," he said simply. "Two of them. And while it was an impressive feat, I have to admit it inconvenienced me. I considered letting you live, but then you came to New York, and I became uncomfortable with how close you came to me. Your second night in the city, you ended up in my home. I could hardly believe it was a coincidence."

"You do not have to do this," I pled. "Write a letter. Sign something. Retract the order."

Albion shook his head. "It is too late. My assassin is already in position. In fact, he might have already struck."

I pulled my brows together, wondering if Albion wasn't losing his clarity as the poison coursed through him. "I'm standing here in front of you. You know I have not been killed yet."

His lips lifted in a smile of pure, sinister amusement. "I was not referring to you, dear. I issued the order for your death in conjunction with another. That of Charles Cresswell. The assassin will be at his house now."

Wet coughs ripped through Albion's chest and this time I saw the blood splatter across the pages on his desk. He tried to catch his breath, but the coughs were coming too fast. When he inhaled, the breaths were shallow, and

I could see the skin around his lips turning purple. Albion Rooker was dying.

"Who is the assassin?" I asked, moving around the desk and taking the papers from Albion's lap. He didn't resist or fight as I took them. He just coughed and stared at me. I shuffled through the pages, but there was no list of assassins like the list of targets. Just information on the targets—names, addresses, family members, places they frequented.

"You will not find anything there," Albion wheezed. When I met his eyes, he tipped his head towards the fireplace and the small pile of ash sitting in the bottom. "I burned it."

The page he'd selected out and burned had been the list of assassins. Albion had confessed to me, but he still had one more secret he wasn't ready to reveal.

Another violent coughing fit claimed his attention, and I no longer cared to stay and talk. Albion Rooker would be dead in a few minutes, but if I was not quick, so might Charles Cresswell.

As I ran from the room, Albion's coughing ceased and was immediately replaced by choking, clawing gasps for air. I heard a large thud like something slamming into the floor, and I thought it might be Albion falling from his chair, but then I closed his front door behind me and ran down the path, leaving him to die alone.

17

P re-dawn had given way to the sunrise since I'd been in Albion's home, and there were considerably more people on the streets than there had been before. People watched and remarked on my odd behavior as I ran from Albion's home and down the street, but I didn't have time to concern myself with their opinions.

I paused just long enough to grab the arm of a passerby. I said that someone was dead or dying in the house behind me, and although I was privately certain the time for medical care was past, I suggested they send for a doctor.

Then, I rushed on without delay. If Albion had been telling the truth, Charles Cresswell was in imminent danger.

I did not allow myself to consider the possibility that I would be too late and Charles was already dead. Charles knew he was being targeted, so perhaps he had been able to overwhelm his attacker the way I had Mr. Barlow in

Simla. Or perhaps, he was fighting off his attacker now, and my arrival would provide an upper hand. I lowered my head and ran faster.

The house, in a similarly nice area, though closer to the street than both Aunt Sarah's and Albion's, was dark. All the curtains were pulled closed and the movement happening on the street as people readied for the start of the day had not yet reached Charles' home. I mounted the stairs and pushed the door open without knocking. Was the fact it was unlocked a sign that I was not the first to arrive?

The house was eerily quiet and nothing like the warm, bright home I'd been in the night before. Just like Albion's, I couldn't hear even a whisper of movement in the entire house, and I did not call out. If possible, I wanted my presence in the home to go unnoticed. Even if Charles had already been killed, the assassin could still be in the house, and I wanted to have surprise on my side.

The doors to the sitting room on the right and dining room on the left were both pulled close, offering no hint of what lay inside the house. So it was that when I unlatched the French door into the dining room and pulled it open, I gasped at the sight beyond it.

Bodies. A servant girl was lying across the arm of a sturdy wooden chair, her thin brown hair covering her face. Another woman had collapsed in the middle of the doorway between the dining room and the kitchen, the swinging door held open against her hip.

I stumbled from the room in surprise, laying a hand over my furiously beating heart. I took several deep

breaths before moving into the room again. If the
servants were dead and the house quiet, there was little
hope for Charles' survival, I knew that. But as I walked
towards the woman on the floor, I noticed the movement
of her chest. Then, I realized there was no blood. I knelt
down next to her and laid a hand on her chest. Her heart
rate was strong and steady, her chest rising and falling as
though asleep rather than dead. I scrambled to the girl
lying across the dining chairs and realized she, too, was
alive and well. Whatever they had been given had simply
made them unconscious.

When I walked into the kitchen, I found another
unconscious body. This woman was lying next to a half-
eaten pastry, her fingers loosely wrapped around the
treat. That was when I noticed a basket of pastries on the
countertop. Without touching anything, I examined the
basket and found a note attached to the handle. *I appreciate all you do for my future husband, and will strive to be a
good mistress when I join the household. Enjoy these pastries
as a sign of my gratitude.*

The handwriting was looping and fanciful, but
although it was signed *Lady Catherine*, it was nothing like
my cousin's neat, regimented script. The note was a fabri-
cation, and I suspected the pastries—or rather, what had
been baked into them—were what caused the servants to
collapse. I slipped the blade from beneath my cardigan
and gripped it in my sweaty palm. It was possible I was
too late and the servants would awaken to realize that,
while they had been unconscious, their employer had
been murdered. But until I knew for certain who was in
the house and who was alive, I would take precautions. I

proceeded blade first from the kitchen and down the servant's hallway towards the rest of the house.

The main floor living areas were empty. I did not see or hear anyone—unconscious, dead, or otherwise. So, carefully, I moved up the central staircase to the second floor. One servant was sprawled across the landing. He was still breathing, though I noted a large bruise forming above his eye. Apparently, he had not eaten the pastries as the other servants had, and the bruise proved that the assassin had already been in the house. Or was still. I took a quiet, calming breath and continued on.

The first room to the right was a private sitting room that was, thankfully, empty, and I moved quickly through it and through the second set of doors that led into the library. The library had a door out to the landing or a second set of doors that led into an office. I could hardly stop spinning in circles, doing my best to cover every entrance and exit in the rooms. There were many places to hide, and I felt woefully unprepared to monitor all of them.

Charles' office, in direct opposition to Albion Rooker's, was orderly and clean. The desk was bare save for a lamp, a fountain pen, and a few decorative pieces that seemed to be awards Charles had accrued throughout his career. I moved around the desk to check beneath it, ensuring Charles was not slumped on the floor, and when I found the chair and floor clear, I loosed a sigh of relief.

Clearly, Albion's assassin had attempted to end Charles' life, but for reasons I did not know, Charles was not home. Perhaps, the assassin left to try again another day, giving me time to warn Charles, convince the police of Albion Rooker's crimes, and put an end to the long chain of deaths that had for so long ruled my life.

I had almost convinced myself that this convenient outcome was not only likely, but probable, when I heard a single footstep in the hallway.

The sound stopped my heart, and I spun towards the door, blade extended. My entire body trembled with fear and anticipation, so much so that it took me a moment to register the familiarity of the sound.

The footstep had not been a simple creak of the floorboards, but rather a sharp tap similar to dance shoes. It was a noise I'd heard before. The night before, actually.

I shook my head, already trying to stave off the realization I was coming to. It could not be true. I did not want it to be true. And yet, I could not deny my own instincts.

"Graham?" I called, my voice wavering with a deep, yearning hope that I was wrong. "Graham, is that you?"

The question was met with silence for several long seconds until the door handle turned with a squeak. And Graham stepped into the office.

18

"Hello, Rose."

I had not seen him since his proposal the night before, and when I'd closed the door between us, he had looked crestfallen and disappointed. But now, Graham's face was split into a cold smile, and his voice was devoid of emotion. He looked and sounded so differently from the kind man I had come to know, that I almost couldn't believe him to be the man I'd met in Simla and crossed the ocean with.

"What are you doing here, Graham?" I asked in hope that his answer would explain everything away. That he would have a good excuse, and our friendship could continue on as expected. However, I knew it would not be so.

As I stood there behind the desk, looking at the man I had come to call a friend, I knew it had all been a lie.

Suddenly, Graham's desire to be close to me, both in Simla and New York, made sense. He had attached himself to me at once and assisted me in my investigation without any questions. At the time, I had attributed it to his affection for me, but now I could see that it was a sense of duty that kept him close to me rather than attraction. That he did not find my requests odd—such as bringing him a curved assassin blade I'd discovered— because it was his role to stay close to me. To monitor my investigation as it progressed.

And then, the night I'd killed Mr. Barlow, I'd gone to the ruins expecting to see Graham waiting for me in his stead. I'd predicted Graham as the assassin, but when I saw Mr. Barlow, I'd assumed I was wrong. It never crossed my mind that there could have been two assassins in the same location.

"I can see in your face that you know the answer," Graham said, his anger thinly veiled. Malice seemed to roll off of him in waves, and I wondered how he had managed to keep it so well contained beneath his friendly façade.

I wanted to cry. And be sick. I was disgusted with myself that not only had I not suspected Graham, I had entertained the idea of marrying him. How could I have been such a fool? Achilles Prideaux had warned me against Graham. He had told me that Graham's attach-ment to me was unusual, but I had counted his suspi-cions as jealousy. Just as I had attributed Graham's strange behavior to his affection for me, I thought Achilles must be so in love with me that it clouded his judgment. When had I become so vain?

"You are an assassin," I stammered, holding the blade steady in front of me. I would not lower it until the fight was over. Until one of us had stopped breathing. Graham had fooled me long enough, and I would not allow it again.

Graham nodded and grinned. "Are you surprised?"

I had to look away. The smile was evil, and yet, too similar to the smile of my friend for me to stomach. It felt as though he was killing the Graham I'd thought I'd known. It felt as though I was mourning a man who had never existed.

"You knew who I was when we met."

He nodded again. "I received word you were to arrive in Simla with the Hutchins', and I made the appropriate connections so we would meet. I must admit, though, I did not expect to earn your trust so easily."

It felt like a slap to the face. Another proof of my incompetence. How could I have been so blind?

"Mr. Barlow was tasked with killing Mr. Hutchins and I was tasked with monitoring you, so our work had a great deal of overlap. He was a great help to me. Until you killed him."

"Before he could kill me," I said, embarrassment and shame turning into anger sharp as a knife. I gripped my blade. "If I was your target, why would Mr. Barlow kill me?"

Graham rolled his eyes. "He was also the man who threw a bomb in the middle of the Simla square. Subtlety did not suit him. Despite my assurances otherwise, he became convinced you were on to him, and he needed to take you out to protect his position. I only followed along to be sure he wouldn't share my secrets and then leave you alive."

I remembered Graham showing up the night I fought

Mr. Barlow amidst the ruins. He'd shown up at the end of the fight, distracting me in the final moments of the battle when Mr. Barlow was closing in. Seeing him had given me comfort at the time. It spurred me on to fight harder, ultimately killing Mr. Barlow. Now, I realized, I had been in more danger than ever. If Mr. Barlow had accidentally let slip Graham's true role, Graham likely would have killed me.

"Mr. Barlow had been in the game too long," Graham said, shaking his head and taking a step towards me. I raised my blade and twisted it towards his heart. He raised an eyebrow, but stopped moving. "Mr. Barlow was suspicious and reckless. He allowed himself to be seen by the locals, and if it had not been you, someone else would have defeated him. He thought too highly of himself and underestimated you. I will not make the same mistake."

"Why wait to kill me?" I asked, side-stepping to the corner of the desk, giving myself more options of escape when Graham grew tired of talk. "We were on the ship to New York together. We've been alone many times since then. Last night, even. Why now?"

"Mr. Barlow's lack of subtlety in killing your father had lasting repercussions," he said coolly. "The police in Simla still believe the attack to have been committed by a local extremist. However, if Mr. Beckingham's daughter turns up dead by suspicious means only a few months after the death of her entire family, people may begin to have doubts."

"So, you were waiting for the right time," I said, remembering Graham's proposal the night before. He had poured his heart out to me, confessing his love and desire to be with me. It had seemed so genuine. I did not for a single second doubt his sincerity. The memory of it sent a shiver through me. "Would the right time have been after we were married?"

Graham's smile flattened. "I must admit your hesitation surprised me. I expected you to accept my offer."

"Perhaps you are not as smart as you think." I would never admit that I had considered it. That, given more time to think, I may have accepted his offer.

Graham ignored me and continued. "When you made a covert visit to Charles' home last night and then did not respond to my proposal of marriage, Albion decided it was time to act. The risk of you uncovering the truth and revealing everything before he was ready was greater than the risk that your death would bring unwanted attention to the Beckingham bombing case. If you had simply accepted my offer, we could be with your family now celebrating the good news rather than here with a knife between us."

He said it as if I was supposed to have regrets. As if I was supposed to want that scenario instead of the current reality. But how could I want that? It would have been a lie. A temporary happiness until Graham found the right time to end my life and remove me as a threat. The romantic attention and proposal had all been meant as a distraction, and I was lucky to be able to say that it had not worked. Rather than dwell on my feelings for Graham, I left and got a confession from Albion Rooker before his death. I would much rather know the truth and be in danger than be unaware of the threat around me.

"But instead," he continued. "I was ordered to kill Charles, and then you. I never believed I'd be so lucky as to kill you both at the same time, however. The servants will be unconscious for several more hours, which should be enough time for Charles to return from wherever he has been."

"I did not love you," I said suddenly, as though it had any power to hurt him. Really, it was my own kind of distraction. I sensed our conversation was coming to an end, and I needed to get closer to the door to the hallway. Graham was standing in front of the double doors that led into the library, but if I could draw him closer to the desk, I could escape into the hallway, down the stairs, and out the front door before he could attack me. It was my only chance at survival.

"Even if I had accepted your proposal," I said, "it never would have been for love. Your Lieutenant façade was dull, and now that I see the man who lies beneath it, I'm even less impressed."

Graham bit his lower lip, and his nostrils flared. Clearly, even though it had all been a lie, he was vainer than he let on. "You seemed to enjoy my company enough."

I shrugged and leaned across the desk towards Graham. He leaned in, as well. "I have secrets of my own, and your company allowed me more freedom than being single would have."

Graham took a step forward, blonde brows furrowed. "You truly believe you have secrets from me? Two trained assassins were watching your every move from the moment you arrived in Simla. I followed you to this very house last night without you being aware. What secrets could you have?"

I raised an eyebrow in a challenge. "Secrets that would change everything."

He took another step forward. Now, he was only one step and an arm's length away. Close enough for me to run, but if he got any closer, that opportunity would slip away. "I don't believe you. Similar to Mr. Barlow, you over-estimate your own abilities. You were not a good enough detective to uncover the truth about me before it was too late, and you are not a good enough liar to keep a secret from a trained assassin."

I inhaled slowly, preparing myself for what was coming next, and then smiled. "And similar to Mr. Barlow, you underestimate me."

Before Graham could speak or move, I took a lunging step out from behind the desk, slashed my knife through the air, and ran. He screamed and hurled himself away from the blade, but I felt it catch on his cheek, and I felt the warmth of blood on my fingers as I ran from the room.

The servant with the bruise on his head was still lying unconscious at the top of the stairs, and the house was dark and quiet except for Graham's stumblings behind me. Though I had surprised him, he would catch up quickly, so I knew I had no time to waste. I ran down the narrow hallway along the stair railing and grabbed the banister to propel myself around the turn and down the stairs. However, before I could, a hand wrapped around my wrist and wrenched me backwards. I yelped and landed on my back, my head bouncing off the hardwood floor, and felt the air knocked from my lungs in a single whoosh.

When I looked up, Graham was leaning over me, one hand pressed to a bleeding wound on his face. His eyes, once crescents turned up in a smile were narrowed into angry slits. He leaned down with his other hand to grab the knife from my hand, and I slashed out again. I caught the material of his jacket, and he fell back, giving me time to rise to my feet. I backed away from him, too out of breath to consider running, the knife held out in front of me.

"I've killed men before," I said, shaking the knife side to side in a warning. "I'll do it again."

Graham's face was red with exertion and embarrassment, and when he lowered his hand, blood flowed down his cheek. "You don't have what it takes to kill someone."

"You saw it," I said. "With Mr. Barlow."

Graham shook his head and took a step forward. I gripped the blade harder, clenching my arms to keep them from trembling. "You stood by while the ruins of an old statue crushed him. You don't know what it is to take a person's life away. To have your own hands be responsible for something like that. Even now, I don't believe you are capable of it."

"I thought you said you wouldn't underestimate me."

Graham smiled, forcing blood from the wound on his cheek, and moved towards me. "And I won't."

He lowered his head and rushed towards me. One of his arms swiped out and connected with my elbow, knocking the knife from my hand. It clattered to the floor and slid towards the wall. I dove towards it, but Graham's body slammed into my side, and we both fell to the floor in a tangle of limbs. His hands wrapped around my arm and my shoulder, and I tried to wriggle out from under him, but it felt as though he was crushing me into the floor. I could feel him moving up steadily, working his way towards my neck. And I knew if he got there, I would lose this fight.

I kicked out at him over and over again until the heel of my shoe finally connected with the center of his leg. He howled in pain and rolled off of me slightly—just enough for me to slide out from under him and grab the knife.

When Graham realized what was happening, he opened his mouth to yell, but the sound died in his throat.

I felt the blade slide between his ribs and heard the catch in his breath when I punctured his lung. He rolled off of me instantly, gripping his side and fighting to rise to his feet. I scrambled away from him, backing up towards the top of the stairs.

Graham had been wrong about me. I could kill a man. And I would in order to save my own life. But that didn't mean I enjoyed it or wanted to. If I could escape without dealing the death blow, I would.

But Graham had other ideas.

He saw me escaping and dragged himself to his knees and then managed to pull himself to standing. He wobbled, blood pulsing from his wound and dripping on the floor as he walked, but his glassy eyes were fixed on me. He would not stop until one of us was dead.

So, knife point first, I charged.

Graham was sluggish from the loss of blood, but he managed to dodge my blade, throwing his body against the stair railing. And that was when I saw my opening. I dropped the knife, spun towards him, and pushed on his chest with both hands. Graham teetered on the edge for a second, eyes wide, hand stretching out for something to stop his fall. But then, he tumbled over the edge and out of view.

All I heard was the crunch of his body against the stairs. And then nothing.

19

I stumbled away from the railing and pressed my back against the wall, too afraid to look over the edge or run down the stairs. What if he wasn't dead? What if he reached out and grabbed my leg as I ran past? I didn't think I'd be able to handle it.

Then, the front door opened.

For a horrifying second, I thought Graham had managed to lift himself to his feet and walk out the front door, but then I heard a scream.

"Is that Graham?" Catherine asked, her voice shrill and panicked.

"Stay away from him," I screamed, pulling myself to my feet and stepping over the servant still sprawled on the stairs.

Catherine and Charles were standing in the doorway, faces pale, eyes wide. Charles had his arm outstretched in front of Catherine, shielding her from any danger that may be coming their way.

"What is going on, Rose?" Charles' eyes darted

around the room, looking for the assassin he suspected was lurking somewhere nearby.

I shook my head. "It's over, Charles. He's dead."

His eyes narrowed, and then he looked at Graham again, understanding falling over him like a fog. "It was Graham?"

"What was Graham?" Catherine asked, pushing Charles' arm away and moving towards the stairs. "What is going on? Is he dead?"

I studied Graham's body, bent in an awkward position, spread across several stairs, blood dripping down them like a water feature. There was a visible wound in the left side of his chest, but it was no longer pulsing blood, and his chest was neither rising nor falling.

"I think so," I said, relief flooding through me. I felt as though I could have collapsed, but I gripped the railing and moved carefully down the stairs, speeding up to pass Graham.

Catherine reached for me the moment I moved off the stairs and pulled me towards the front door, her eyes assessing me. "Are you hurt? Is anyone else hurt?"

Charles ran past us to where the servant was lying on the stairs.

"They are only unconscious," I said over my shoulder. "Graham gave them something to put them to sleep."

"I must telephone a doctor," he said, running back down the stairs and into the sitting room.

"And the police," I reminded him.

Catherine looked at both of us as though we were crazy and then stepped away from me, crossing her arms over her chest. "What is going on? Why do you two act like this isn't a surprise?"

Charles stopped but didn't look at his fiancé, instead focusing his attention on the floor. Catherine glared at him for a moment before turning her attention to me.

"Rose," she said sternly.

I opened my mouth and then closed it, unsure what the right words were. Before I could find them, Charles spun on his heel and moved to Catherine, grabbing her shoulders. In a rush of words and emotion, he explained everything. The deaths of his colleagues, the threatening note, the paranoia and fear that she could be hurt because of her connection to him. Catherine listened without moving, and I simply rested against the banister, too exhausted to leave the room and give them privacy. When Charles finished, he released Catherine and took a step away, waiting for her response.

She paused for a moment and then whipped out at him with her hand, slapping his arm once and then again. "How could you not tell me something like this, Charles? I worried you didn't love me anymore. I thought you were going to cancel our wedding."

"The information was dangerous," Charles said, backing away, arms lifted to defend himself.

Catherine pressed her lips into a thin line and then turned her attention to me. "And you. I asked you here to help me. Why would you not tell me what was going on?"

"I made her swear not to," Charles said, giving me an apologetic smile over Catherine's shoulder.

"I am your cousin," Catherine argued. "You should have told me."

I nodded. "Yes, I should have. I'm sorry."

The apology seemed to make her more upset. She could no longer direct her anger at me, so she turned back to her husband-to-be. "And I am going to be your wife, Charles Cresswell. Should you ever again find yourself the target of an assassin, please tell me."

"All right," Charles said, nodding. "I will."

Catherine huffed out a breath, her shoulders sagging, and then in the next breath, she was sobbing. Charles rushed forward and wrapped his arms around her, pressing her cheek into his chest.

"You could have died," she sobbed.

He patted her hair and kissed her forehead. "But I didn't. Thanks to you, in fact. If you had not come early this morning to force me on a walk, I might have been here when Graham arrived."

The thought brought another sob out of Catherine, and then all at once, she broke away from Charles, wiped her eyes, and turned to me. "Oh, Rose. I'm so sorry. You must be devastated."

I waved away her concern. "It's all right. Really."

"He proposed to you," Catherine said, head tilting to the side, pity etched into her features.

"I was going to say no," I said, as though this solved everything. It didn't, of course. But at least my family would not believe I had been in love with him. I couldn't bear that.

Unable to take another second of my cousin's pity, I stood up and marched back up the stairs, ignoring the incredible urge to flee that rose up as I neared Graham's body.

"What are you doing?" Charles asked. When I didn't answer, he sighed and remembered his earlier mission. "I'm going to fetch the doctor. And the police."

The blood beneath Graham was already darkening and growing thick, but his body was warm when I reached inside his jacket. Immediately, my fingers found what I'd hoped they would. I pulled the small packet of neatly folded pages—now stained with blood—from his jacket and retreated down the stairs.

"What is that?" Catherine asked.

"Proof," I said, holding the letter up. "At least, I hope. Graham was working under the leadership of Albion Rooker."

Catherine gasped, but I didn't pause long enough for her to respond.

"Albion Rooker is dead, and he made it sound as though he intended his plan to be made public. Graham seemed the most likely person to reveal the details, and I believe these—" I held up the bloodied papers. "Are the details."

Catherine nodded slowly, her fingers twisting nervously in front of her, and then she lunged at me. Her arms were around my neck before I could register what was happening, and she buried her face into my neck.

"I'm so glad you are not hurt," she said, her body trembling. "I would never have been able to forgive myself if you had come to New York and been killed trying to help me."

"I would have been killed if I'd stayed in Simla," I said, grabbing her shoulders and holding her at arm's length. I looked earnestly into her blue eyes. "You bringing me to New York saved my life Catherine. Without you, I would still count Graham as a friend."

She took a shuddering breath. "So, you are not angry with me?"

It was strange to see Catherine so vulnerable. Since meeting her, I'd imagined her an impenetrable force of strength, independent of anyone else's approval. But since coming to New York, I'd seen a softer side of her. The side I now knew was only revealed to those she trusted. I felt honored to be amongst their number.

"Never," I said, twining my arm through hers and leading her into the sitting room. "You asked me for help, and I agreed. Anything that happened after that was simply the danger of having dear friends."

She started and turned to me. "We are friends?"

"Aren't we?" I asked, bumping her with my hip.

She rolled her eyes but could not stop herself from smiling. "I supposed we are."

We sat down together side-by-side on the sofa, talking as we waited for the police to arrive.

20

Alice draped herself over the arm of the sofa, one arm thrown across her forehead like a model from a Renaissance painting. "I can't believe it is almost time to leave. Do we have to go?"

"Of course, we have to go," Catherine snapped, annoyed with her sister's dramatics. "I'm getting married. You were excited about it a few weeks ago."

Alice lifted her arm and sat up long enough to glare at her sister before falling back into mourning. "That was a few weeks ago. Now, I have to say goodbye, and I'm not ready."

"The boy—whatever his name is—hasn't been to the house in over a week," Catherine said.

"I thought you asked him to stop coming over last week," I said. "So you would 'have more time to pack.'"

Alice groaned at both of us. "Neither of you know anything about love."

"I'm the one getting married," Catherine said, throwing her arms up in defeat.

"And I'm the one who was almost engaged to a murderer," I said flatly.

Alice's cheeks reddened, embarrassed at her slip, and Catherine bit her lip. It had been two weeks since the final fight with Graham, and no one seemed to know how to discuss it with me. So, I'd taken it upon myself to bring it up.

"I'm fine," I said.

"Are you?" Alice asked, looking at me like I was a china cup with a cracked handle.

"Yes," I said firmly. "It is all over now. I'm happy to put it all behind me."

Alice's lips twisted to one side of her mouth, looking unsure, but Catherine winked at me. It was still strange to count her as one of my best friends, but it was strange in a delightful kind of way. She was the only person I'd told about my conflicting feelings about Graham. I was not proud of how badly I'd misread his character, but on some level, I did miss him. Or, at least, I missed the idea of his company. The comfort of having someone who cared about me more than anyone else. It was a nice thought.

Since I'd unraveled the mystery of 'The American,' Charles had become a close confidante, too. After reading through the papers I'd found in Graham's coat pocket—which turned out to be a list of the assassins employed by The American and the targets they killed —I'd been able to assure myself that all of the assassins were dead and the intricate plot was truly over. I then handed the information over to Charles, knowing he had the connections to make the information known to the right people. Finally, everyone would know the true reason the Beckinghams had been murdered. The world would know that General Hughes had not committed suicide, but had actually been murdered. All of the family members of the other victims would finally have the justice they deserved. It was a nice feeling.

"Well, good," Alice said, as though that settled that. She still looked dubious, but she also seemed willing to take me at my word to avoid the subject. "Because a wedding is meant to be a joyful occasion."

"I thought you were in mourning," Catherine teased. "Over your American beau. What was his name?"

Alice sat up, smoothing her dress down over her legs, and shook her head. "I am not in mourning over him, precisely. Merely at the loss of what could have been."

"Ah," Catherine mocked, one eyebrow raised. "Of course. That makes perfect sense."

"So, I assume you will be attending Catherine's wedding alone, then?" I asked. "Since you will still be in mourning."

"Will you wear all black?" Catherine asked. "That will clash with the color scheme, but we would all understand."

Alice stood up and stomped her foot, looking more like the child I'd first met a year before. "I preferred it when the two of you didn't speak."

Catherine threw her head back and laughed, but I reached out and grabbed Alice as she tried to stomp out of the room. "I'm sorry. We will not tease you anymore."

"We won't?" Catherine asked, looking disappointed.

Then, she saw the fire in Alice's eyes and sighed. "I mean, yes, Rose is right. We will stop teasing you."

Alice looked at us both suspiciously for a moment before her face split into a smile and she dropped down onto the sofa. "I actually have several options for an escort to the wedding."

"How?" Catherine asked, shocked. "You haven't been in London for months."

"I've been corresponding with several boys back home."

"You flirt!" Catherine shouted, mouth agape.

Aunt Sarah walked into the room, a servant following her with a tray of tea and biscuits. "Are you talking about me, dear?"

"Of course not," Catherine laughed.

"Good," she said. "Because I danced with five different men at the party the other night, but three of them were married and the other two I had no interest in. Even widows deserve a turn on the dance floor."

"Apparently, Alice has been writing multiple boys back in London," Catherine explained.

"Alice," Aunt Sarah said, clicking her tongue. "Does Daniel know about these European boys?"

"Daniel!" I said, lifting a finger like I'd solved the case. "That was his name."

Alice grabbed a biscuit and flopped back on the sofa. "His name does not matter. I am not the one engaged. I made no promises to him, nor he to me. Besides, I can't rightfully carry on a relationship with an American all the way from London."

"Will you stay in London after the wedding?" Aunt Sarah asked, sipping her tea.

The question brought the conversation to a stall. Alice turned to her aunt, biting her lip. "I think so."

Aunt Sarah set down her cup and patted Alice's knee. "Do not look at me like I'm some wounded bird. I've lived alone for many years, and I will continue to do so after you are gone."

Suddenly, Alice leaned forward and wrapped her arms around her aunt. "I know, but I will miss you. I'm not ready to say goodbye."

"Yes, your kindness has been unmatched, Aunt Sarah," Catherine said, smiling sadly.

Aunt Sarah pointed a warning finger at Catherine. "Now, you are moving back to New York with your husband after the wedding, so do not get emotional with me. And I'm sure Alice and Rose will come visit, so I will see you all again."

As Alice began planning out the next several years' worth of transatlantic visits, I couldn't help but imagine what the future would hold for me. Upon arriving in New York City, I'd had a feeling of finally returning home. I couldn't imagine going back to London. But the city was different from my memories. The life I'd had in New York could never be again. And moreover, I didn't think I wanted that life anymore.

Over it all, though, Achilles Prideaux stuck out in my mind like a thorn in my heel. No matter how I tried to navigate around him, my attention returned to what role he would play in my life upon my return to London.

Because he knew the truth about my identity, I did

not have to lie to him. However, the question I would have to answer was who I wanted to be. Nellie Dennet from New York City or Rose Beckingham from London?

"Rose?"

I looked up to see Catherine, Alice, and Aunt Sarah all staring at me, eyes wide and expectant.

"Sorry?" I asked, confused.

"Aunt Sarah asked what your plans are now," Catherine said gently.

"Will you stay in London or are you setting off for another adventure?" Aunt Sarah asked with a smile.

Achilles Prideaux's face appeared in my mind once again, and I knew I would not be able to push him away forever. The time was coming when I would have to make a choice.

"I truly do not know," I said honestly. I reached out and grabbed Catherine's hand, squeezing her fingers. "Right now, I just want to see my beautiful cousin get married."

Catherine grinned at me, and Alice rolled her eyes, still annoyed with our blossoming friendship.

"You still have some weeks left to think about it," Alice said. "The wedding isn't happening tomorrow, you know."

"Which means you have some weeks left to think, too," I said.

Alice drew her brows together. "Think about what?"

"About which of your many suitors you're going to take to my wedding," Catherine said.

Alice stomped out of the room, grabbing another

biscuit on her way, while Catherine and I laughed. Even Aunt Sarah was biting her lip.

Sitting there with my family, a few weeks seemed like a lifetime away.

*Continue following the mysterious adventures of Rose
Beckingham in
"A Final Rest."*

ABOUT THE AUTHOR

Blythe Baker is a thirty-something bottle redhead from the South Central part of the country. When she's not slinging words and creating new worlds and characters, she's acting as chauffeur to her children and head groomer to her household of beloved pets.

Blythe enjoys long walks with her dog on sweaty days, grubbing in her flower garden, cooking, and ruthlessly de-cluttering her overcrowded home. She also likes binge-watching mystery shows on TV and burying herself in books about murder.

To learn more about Blythe, visit her website and sign up for her newsletter at www.blythebaker.com